THE LOST BOY

A DETECTIVE MARK TURPIN CRIME THRILLER

RACHEL AMPHLETT

CHAPTER ONE

Run.

Matthew Arkdale gritted his teeth as his ankle rolled, then stumbled and kept going.

His breath escaped his lips in gasps, the cold October breeze slapping at his ears and cheeks while he ran past a bright yellow security barrier and pushed a middle-aged man out of his way.

He ignored the glare from the security crew loitering at the fringes of the crowd. The man's loud curse was lost within seconds, drowned amongst a cacophony of shouts from the people lining the street and cluttering the road.

Don't look back.

There were no vehicles here, no risk of being run over. The whole of the town centre had been closed off for the fair, save for a scant number of diversion routes that snaked around the periphery.

His pace slowed to a fast walk – the pavement was cluttered by parents with pushchairs and toddlers, teenagers walking four abreast in the middle of the street, older people strolling at leisure.

A thumping bass accompanied the roar of a commentator over the heads of the people in front of him, calling them to the more expensive rides, the ones with spiralling metalwork that curled up into the night sky and carried the screams of excited thrill seekers across the town centre.

A prickling sensation crawled between his shoulders and up his spine, settling at the base of his neck. Goosebumps spread across his arms, the fine hairs itching against the long-sleeved sports top he wore under his hooded sweatshirt.

Eyes darting left then right, he threaded his way between a couple with twin boys next to the dodgems, the kids bickering about which coloured car they wanted to ride in, and then ducked into a side street.

A gloom enveloped him, a blanket of grey light that made him blink to counteract the night blindness caused by the bright lights of the rides over his shoulder.

Stumbling into the covered doorway of one of the Regency houses that crowded the narrow road, Matthew leaned forward and rested his hands on his knees, panting. His lungs ached from the effort to stay ahead of his pursuer – a deep pain that wracked his chest and was echoed by the pounding of his heart.

A heaving sigh escaped his lips as he peered towards the throng lining the main street.

He had no idea where he was, where to go, or what to do next.

This wasn't his town.

He had never seen the man until this morning – but he knew.

Knew now that coincidence had nothing to do with spotting him a second time only moments before his eyes had widened in recognition.

Moments before, Matthew had seen the knife in the man's hand and fled.

Shaking from hunger, fear, and the damp chill that seeped through his clothing, he held his breath as the man appeared at the apex to the T-junction, one side of his face in shadow, the other a flickering concoction of colour caused by the strobing lights from the funhouse to the left of the street.

Voices, similar in age to his, rang out within the four-storey structure as they navigated sloping floors and rope bridges while calling down to their parents from barriers that prevented them from falling out of the windows carved into the painted frontage.

The man sniffed the air, then moved away out of sight.

A hollowness permeated Matthew's slight frame as he cowered back into the shadows, fatigued. He blinked to counteract a sudden dizziness that seized his vision, and clenched his teeth as a painful cramp clawed at his stomach.

He cried out at a movement behind the door where he cowered, voices on the other side reaching his ears before the latch turned.

He couldn't stay here.

Keep moving.

Matthew flipped up the hood of his sweatshirt, pulled it forward until it left his features in shadow, then shoved his hands in his pockets and jogged along the pavement until he was level with the main thoroughfare once more.

The noise assaulted his ears, numbing his senses and creating a disorientation that unnerved him.

A young child, no more than six years old, started bawling beside a stall offering prizes of soft toys, her teary gaze watching as a pink helium-filled balloon, having escaped her grasp, lifted into the air. Her cries of anguish blended with an argument that broke out between four teenagers queuing for the gravity wheel ride, the raised voices making him jump as he passed.

He lowered his chin, ignoring the cat-calls that trailed in his wake as he became the new focus for the teenagers' disdain, and pushed into the shadows cast by the dimmed lights of a home interiors shop closed up for the night.

Pausing a moment, he craned his neck and peered amongst the crowd but the man who was hunting him was nowhere to be seen.

A cheer rose from another stall, the sound effects from a laser gun game driving him forward with a renewed urgency.

Run.

Hunkered low, his slight frame weaving left and right, he negotiated the busy street and dodged around discarded coffee cups and soft drink cans.

The road widened out into a marketplace, and Matthew turned his attention to the children's rides that crowded the uneven cobblestones. A long line of people encircled a brightly lit carousel, jostling for space beside a large roundabout with teacups for seats.

He passed by all of it, his thoughts a blur as his fingers wrapped around the small bag in his left pocket. He could feel the hard round pills pushing against the plastic, and swallowed to lose the sour taste in his mouth.

It had seemed like a good idea at the time.

Easy money.

Freedom.

A sense of taking back control of his life.

And now look at him – a fugitive, on the run in a town where he had no friends, and pursued by someone who would kill him, of that he had no doubt.

The entrance to an alleyway caught his eye, a

darkened maw that led out of the market square, away from the bright lights and noise.

Matthew shot a glance over his shoulder, saw no-one observing his movements, and ran the final few metres to reach it.

The shadows welcomed him, the neon lights trailing after his silhouette until he outpaced them.

He winced as a stitch tore into his ribs, and slowed to a walking pace, his breathing laboured.

Don't stop.

A groan escaped his lips as he passed a side door into the café that bordered one side of the alleyway, the sound of a radio playing carrying through the woodwork.

He was so damn tired.

Exhausted.

Scared.

Three large industrial-sized bins lined the wall opposite the doorway and Matthew edged past them, gagging at the stench of rotten food and waste.

The fine hairs on the back of his neck prickled a split second before he heard the voice.

'Where d'you think you're running to, Matty?'

He threw himself against the wall behind the last bin and brought his fist to his mouth, holding his breath in a desperate attempt to conceal his whereabouts.

Heavy footsteps approached, the man unhurried.

Run.

I can't, he thought.

I'm tired.

I want to go home.

Except he couldn't, could he?

There was no home.

The footsteps drew closer.

He could hear the man breathing, hard.

'Come out, Matty. There's nowhere to go. Doesn't matter if you run. We'll find you. *He'll* find you…'

He could smell him before he saw him – a fetid stink of unwashed clothing, body odour, sweat.

Matthew gagged, then broke cover.

He didn't stand a chance.

The man reached out, snatched hold of the back of his jacket and jerked him to a standstill.

A burst of pain shot into his back, driving into skin and muscle, burning into sinew.

Crying out, Matthew gritted his teeth, his heart pounding as he squirmed and tried to loosen the man's grip.

It was no use – his attacker was older, bigger, stronger.

Desperate.

The man let him go for a moment, then placed a heavy hand on his shoulder and spun him around until they faced each other.

His eyes widened in fear as the man raised the knife, his lips peeling back to reveal rotten teeth. He took a step back, tried to wriggle away, tried to escape…

The knife plunged into his stomach, fire spreading up into his ribcage.

Then the man shoved him away as if he couldn't bear to touch him, and Matthew was falling backwards.

Fine mist clung to his hair, a shocked breath escaping his lips in a cloud of condensation as the warmth left his lungs.

It hurts.

A single tear rolled over his cheek, the salty

water tracing its way across the grime that slicked his skin.

Matthew's knees buckled, his legs shaking moments before his shoulder crashed against the hard pavement.

Then, darkness.

CHAPTER TWO

The twelve-year-old girl leapt back and emitted a strangled scream at the sight of the skull's grinning jaw.

Flashes of light blinded her vision, highlighting the criss-cross of bones that lay under the skull, arranged so that she could spot the ribs, the fingers, the legs.

A pumping beat thundered in the air, decibel levels thumping in her chest and deadening her senses from all but the nightmare vision that lurched from the shadows.

Shivering, eyes wide with terror and oblivious to the light rain that peppered her slight frame, she blinked, and then swallowed as the skull's jaw opened wide and laughter cackled from a speaker above her head.

Behind her, a chorus of screams pierced the night, and a hand wrapped around her arm.

Her sister's voice bellowed in her ear.

'I can't believe you fell for that.'

Anna turned away from the animated display welcoming people to the ghost train ride, forcing a smile at her older sibling. 'I wasn't expecting it, that's all.'

'Yeah, right.'

'Stop teasing her, Louise.' Detective Sergeant Mark Turpin reached out his hand for his younger daughter. 'All right, Anna?'

'I'm fine.' Her voice defiant, she glared at her older sibling and shrugged off his touch.

'Did you want to have a go on this ride?'

'No. I was just looking.'

'Right, then. I'm starving. Who wants hot dogs?'

'I do.' Lucy O'Brien grinned at Anna, and then pointed to the scruffy dog at her heels. 'And I'll bet Hamish won't say no to a sausage, either.'

Anna's face brightened as the dog tugged at

his lead, and Louise rolled her eyes before holding up her phone to snap a photograph of the colourful fairground rides along the road beside them.

Mark paused to let the two girls go ahead, then winked at Lucy. 'Disaster avoided.'

She laughed, slipped her hand into his and gave it a squeeze.

The aroma of onions cooking on an open grill teased his taste buds, his stomach rumbling as they followed the two girls towards a line of catering wagons that had been parked outside a busy pub. Ruing the diet he had been trying to maintain since the summer, he ran a hand over black curly hair and sighed.

At thirty-eight, he was all too aware of his forties approaching and with it all the health issues he could see in many of his older colleagues.

'You're thinking too hard,' said Lucy over the noise of the crowd. 'I can hear the cogs whirring from here.'

He pointed to the prices listed on a blackboard next to the Ferris wheel. 'It was only fifty pence when I was their age.'

'It's called inflation,' she said, and grinned. 'Think yourself lucky we came tonight – they put up the prices on some of the rides at the Michaelmas Fair on Tuesday last week. Anyway, I saw your face on the waltzer earlier – you're enjoying yourself.'

He smiled, conceding the point, and then they reached the front of the food queue and he decided to stop worrying about the cost of everything. His daughters were here, they were having fun – and if the size of the burger Anna held in her hand was any indication, they were hungry.

'Move over here, out of the way,' he said, leading them to the doorway of a darkened clothing store. 'Does anyone want to go on the dodgems after this?'

Louise wrinkled her nose. 'Dad, we haven't been on those since we were little. What about the big swing at the end of the street instead? We could walk back there.'

A shiver ran down Mark's spine at the memory of the tiny swings suspended on top of an enormous rotating pole, and he shook his head.

'Maybe next year. Anna needs to be a bit

taller. Mind you, the way that burger's just disappeared, it isn't going to take long before she grows.'

That raised a laugh, and his youngest daughter hiccupped before balling up her paper napkin and shoving it in her pocket.

He finished his hot dog, held out the last morsel for Hamish, and then wiped his fingers. 'Okay, time for one more ride at this end of the street, and then we'll head home. You two might have an early holiday pass from school, but you still have homework to hand in tomorrow morning, right?'

'Thanks for the reminder, Dad,' said Louise, scowling.

He shook his head as she flounced away from the doorway, Anna in tow as they worked their way towards Market Place, and then felt Lucy's arm loop through his.

'Cheer up,' she said. 'When she was helping me wash up after lunch, she told me how good it was to be spending some time with you.'

'Really?' He'd taken the girls to visit Lucy on her narrowboat, and they hadn't stopped talking about it all afternoon. 'That's good to know. Anna seems happy enough, but it's hard to tell what's going around in Louise's head sometimes.'

'Well, I'm sure she knows she can talk to you if she needs to. Have you heard from Debbie?'

'She's arrived in St Helier and called me when she got back to the hotel after going to the hospital.'

'How's her mother?'

Mark shrugged. 'Not good. She had a stroke, and they're still trying to work out what damage has been caused.'

Lucy murmured a response, and then froze as a piercing scream cut through the noise from the fairground rides.

It rang out over the excited shouts and screeches from the rides, different in pitch, and full of terror.

Mark craned his neck, spotted his daughters a few metres ahead, and hurried to join them.

'Dad?' Anna's voice wobbled.

He held up his hand to silence her, straining his ears to hear over the thudding bass-heavy music from the ride next to him.

Then he saw her – a woman in her late twenties, bundled up in a dark-coloured anorak

THE LOST BOY   17

against the elements, running from an alleyway beside a café.

Another scream carried on the breeze.

Mark watched as the woman tore across the cobblestones, weaving between the carousel and swings before she reached one of the security personnel and began pointing towards the direction from which she had appeared.

He frowned as the security guard paled and brought a radio to his lips.

'Lucy? Can you wait here with the girls?'

She pushed her curls from her face, her eyes quizzical. 'Of course. Why?'

'I want to find out what's going on. Back in a minute.'

He didn't wait for an answer, and instead strode to intercept the woman and the security guard as the pair pushed through the tide of people flooding the market square.

Her eyes wide in shock, the woman kept one hand on the security guard's arm as she led him towards the entrance to the alleyway.

Mark caught up with them beside the carousel, ignored the children's excited cries as the machine spun them around, and cupped his hands around his warrant card.

'DS Mark Turpin, Thames Valley Police. What's going on?'

'There's a boy in the alleyway,' said the woman, her voice catching in a sob that wracked her body. 'He's been stabbed. I think he's dead.'

CHAPTER THREE

Loud music and excited shouts from the rides merged into a white noise that filled Mark's ears, creating a vacuum as his mind processed the woman's words.

Oblivious to the colourful procession of umbrellas that were being raised into the air as drizzle turned into a shower, he ran through all the possible scenarios in his head, and then—

'Have you phoned for an ambulance?' he said, pulling out his mobile phone.

She hugged her arms to her sides. 'I-I'm sorry. No. There's so much blood…'

'Did you check if he was breathing?'

The woman shook her head, eyes wide.

'What's your name?

'Clare. Clare Baxter. I work in the café.'

'And you're…?'

'S-Simon Carmichael,' said the security guard, his voice shaking.

'Clare, how far along the alleyway is he?'

'About halfway. The service door opens out next to those bins. I was putting out the rubbish, and the light from the kitchen—'

'Wait here, both of you.'

Mark hit the dial button, gave his credentials and requested an ambulance and a uniformed patrol to attend the scene, then shoved his phone in his pocket and squinted into the darkness of the alleyway, aiming the light from his phone at the ground.

Hurrying forwards, he could see the open door from the café swinging in the wind that buffeted him along and ruffled his hair. The bins Clare had described were lined against one side of the wall, leaving a narrow gap on the left. Beyond those, streetlights shone at the end of the alleyway.

Nothing moved.

No-one called out.

Holding his phone aloft, he swept the beam back and forth, his mouth dry. He pushed the door closed so he could pass easily, and then strained his ears over the thumping music. The light from his phone swept past the bins next to the door, across the ground – and then picked out a crumpled form lying further along.

The teenager was dressed in a hoodie and jeans, his feet covered with off-white branded sneakers.

'Christ.'

Mark dropped to a crouch, took one look at the pool of blood under the slight form, and then pulled aside the hood that partially covered the boy's face.

Shock ricocheted through his body as he took in the pale features obscured by blood that had smeared across the boy's cheek, followed by a desperate urge to make this right. He took in the closed eyes and reached out with his fingers to check for a pulse.

Nothing.

'Shit.'

Placing his phone on the concrete beside him, he turned the boy so he lay flat on his back, clasped his hands together, and began chest compressions.

He raised his gaze to the boy's face and frowned at a memory that nagged at the fringes of his thoughts. Adjusting his hands, his movements followed a beat that had been drilled into him at regular first aid sessions.

Sirens wailed in the distance, creating an eerie backdrop to the pulsating bass from the rides beyond the alley.

As sweat began to bead at his forehead, Mark's breaths became ragged while he tried to maintain the same rhythm.

'Come on, come on.'

He paused a moment, holding his fingers to the boy's neck, before continuing with a renewed urgency.

His stomach contracted as a stark reality set in, and then there were voices at the end of the alleyway, shouted commands, running footsteps.

A firm hand gripped his shoulder. 'We'll take it from here.'

Mark staggered backwards, exhausted, and leaned against the café door while the two paramedics swept into action.

He tried to tune into their murmured conversation as the boy's sweatshirt was snipped away, exposing a faded T-shirt that soon met the same fate, and then watched as his body jolted with the shock from the defibrillator.

'He's been stabbed,' said one of the paramedics over his shoulder.

'Any sign of the weapon?'

'No.'

Mark hauled himself away from the wall and stood beside him as his colleague sat back on his heels and shook his head.

'Sorry, mate.'

Blood rushed in Mark's ears as he took in the pitiful figure lying at his feet, and he reached out, placing his hand on the side of the bin to steady himself.

'Thanks for trying,' he said, his training taking over. 'Get yourselves to the end of the alleyway. I'm closing this off as a crime scene.'

He followed in their wake, grateful to see two uniformed constables hovering at the entrance to Market Place.

Beyond the small crowd of professionals grouped beside the abandoned tables outside the café's entrance, a few passers-by walked past with children in tow, the kids' attention on the rides while the adults gaped with open mouths at the scene unfolding in the square.

'Get a cordon set up,' said Mark to the two officers. He turned to the security guard. 'I'll need you to help coordinate until I get more help.'

The man nodded. 'Anything you need.'

'Okay. Stay away from the alley, but anything else these two ask you to do, please follow their instructions.'

After ensuring they taped off both the entrance from their position near the rides as well as the rear exit from the alleyway that led to the loading areas for the shops, and arranging for additional backup, he checked the signal on his phone then dialled a name from the contacts list.

'Sarge?'

Detective Constable Jan West's voice bubbled through a background noise that sounded similar to that near Mark.

'Where are you?'

'The boys are on the dodgems. I heard sirens.'

'Can you get yourself along to Market Place? We've got a fatal stabbing.'

'Bloody hell.'

She lowered the phone, and he recognised the voice in the background as that of her husband, Scott. Then she was back.

'I'll be right there.'

He hung up, and then heard a familiar voice.

'Dad!'

Mark's head snapped around at Anna's call, to see his two daughters beside Lucy, frightened expressions on their young faces.

He followed Anna's stare, taking in his bloodied hands, his stained jacket and trousers.

His shoulders slumped.

Hurrying across the square towards them, ignoring the shocked stares from passers-by, he shoved his phone in his pocket and tried to work out what he was going to say.

'Is someone dead?' said Louise, stepping forward, her brow furrowed.

Mark nodded. His daughters were no strangers to what his job entailed, and he would never lie to them.

'Yes. A teenager.'

'Was it an accident?' Anna's eyes were wide as she peered up at him.

'I don't think so.' He turned his gaze to Lucy, but she shook her head.

'The girls can stay with me tonight. I've got plenty of spare bedding. They can have my bed, and I'll sleep in the cabin.'

'I'm sorry—'

'It's okay, don't worry.' She forced a smile and placed an arm around Anna. 'That all right with you two? Shall we head back to mine and let your dad do his job?'

Louise reached out for his arm and squeezed it. 'We'll be fine, Dad. Lucy's right.'

His throat tightened at the sincerity in her voice, at the thought of the dead boy in the alleyway who must surely be the same age as her, and fought back the tears that pricked at his eyes.

They were both so young.

He didn't know what he would do if he lost them.

Kissing his daughter's cheek, he hugged Anna, and then managed a smile as Lucy squeezed his arm.

'I'll wait up for you.'

'Thank you.'

He watched as the three of them wove their

way between the rides, Hamish at their heels, until they were gone from sight and then turned at the sound of footsteps hurrying towards him.

Jan West sounded out of breath, but she was here, and she was ready if the look on her face was anything to go by.

'Are you all right?' she said as she joined him.

'It's a kid, Jan. A teenage boy.'

CHAPTER FOUR

Half an hour later, the café had been closed, and Clare Baxter's statement taken.

Jan sent the woman home after making sure there was someone available if she needed to talk, before turning her attention to the police officers maintaining the cordon that stretched from the corner of Bury Street and around the back of the children's rides.

She pulled up her coat hood against the persistent rain that filled the air and tried to ignore the stream of parents hurrying past with their children in tow, the adults wearing frightened expressions as news spread about the boy's murder, while the kids were having tantrums at their night out being cut short.

Turning away, she raised her gaze to the flickering lights and neon signs that flashed above her head, the cheerful colours strobing against the buildings a stark contrast to the blue lights from the emergency vehicles crowding the entrance to the High Street.

The aroma of candy floss and doughnuts wafted on the breeze that chased the rain, a cloying smell that turned her stomach.

Her phoned pinged, and she glanced down at the screen. A message from Scott, to say he and the boys were home and that he'd get them to school in the morning.

She shoved it back in her pocket, thoughts of her own children tumbling together with the pitiful sight of the reversing lights from the coroner's vehicle at the far end of the alleyway before it braked to a standstill near the exit.

A group of journalists huddled at one end of the cordon, far enough away from the alleyway to alleviate the risk of any photographs being obtained that could be shared online within moments, and a drone operator had already been given short shrift.

While she continued to walk around the perimeter of the square, the crime scene investigation team began erecting a screen at the end of the alleyway and a white tent was manhandled into place to afford them privacy while they worked.

Over on the far side of the square, Turpin had his mobile phone to his ear, his face grim as he relayed an update to Detective Inspector Ewan Kennedy, his finger in his other ear as he tried to block out the noise around him.

One by one, rides in the Market Place ground to a standstill as the square filled with uniformed officers and security guards.

They had done their best in difficult circumstances, creating a funnel from the steel security barriers that had been used to block off traffic from the town centre. Now, the public had to pass through it in order to leave the square so that names and contact details could be gleaned before sending them away into the night.

Tempers had frayed, frustration bubbling to the surface of some people until a murmured response from one of the officers implied that someone had died. Their expressions turned from indignant to horrified to chastened, their heads bowed as they scurried away.

Panic threatened – Jan had never dealt with so many potential witnesses, so many ways in which a killer could disappear into a crowd or leave the scene via streets that were dark compared to the snaking line of fairground rides along Ock Street.

She gave herself a mental shake, and continued her circuit of Market Place, noting where CCTV and privately owned cameras were placed, creating a list of businesses that would have to be contacted in the morning. To this, she added the name of a bank's logo displayed across the top of an ATM in the hope that something might be caught on that camera to help the ensuing investigation.

Her uniformed colleagues would walk the routes from the square and carry out a similar exercise, but she wanted a head start.

A voice called her name, and she turned to see Turpin approaching.

'Jasper has cleared a path to the crime scene. Do you want to walk it with me?'

Following him back to the cordon, she dipped under the blue and white tape after scrawling her signature on a form and handing back the clipboard to a young plainclothed officer with traces of face paint on her cheeks.

She saw a flicker of recognition in the woman's eyes. 'Were you here with your kids, too?'

'Yes. Sent them home with my mum as soon as I heard. Figured I'd try to help.'

Jan clenched her teeth as the tall CSI lead handed her a pair of coveralls and bootees to cover her shoes, then followed Turpin as Jasper pulled the screen aside and led the two detectives to the scene of the boy's death.

'I didn't hold out much hope for him,' said Turpin, his voice breaking. He coughed, then said, 'There was too much blood. I checked for a pulse, then tried CPR before the ambulance arrived. He didn't stand a chance.'

Jan swallowed.

A few metres ahead, the coroner's team zipped closed a sleek body bag and hoisted the victim onto a gurney. They wheeled it away without a backward glance.

Despite the businesslike way the two men busied themselves loading the gurney into the back of the van at the end of the alleyway, she knew they would be affected by the teenager's murder.

They all were, particularly when a death involved one so young.

'Did you find the weapon used to stab him?'

Jasper shook his head. 'Nothing yet. We've extended our search into the road beyond the alley, though – there are more bins for the shops that need to be checked for a start.'

'I'll have a word with uniform and request a search of bins along the roads leading from the town centre as well,' said Turpin. 'They can coordinate with your team if anything comes up.'

Jan let their voices wash over her as she took in the dark stain on the ground, now floodlit by high arc lamps that the CSI team had erected on tripods to assist in their work.

'How old do you think he was?' she said.

'Thirteen, maybe fourteen,' said Turpin.

Jan exhaled as she ran her eyes over the blood stains that trailed away to the rear of the alleyway.

'So, he was attacked, and then didn't make it far enough to get help.'

'Looks that way,' said Jasper. He pointed to where a second team of CSIs worked. 'There's a lot of blood nearer the café's bins that would indicate where he was stabbed, with the resulting blood from both the wound and the weapon used. We've got a smear on the wall just over there, as if he got that far after being stabbed and paused to steady himself before trying to make his way to the rear of the alley.'

'Except he didn't, and died here.' Turpin's head was lowered, his mouth set as he looked at the floor. 'Any way of identifying him?'

'No identification,' said Jasper. He put out a hand to a colleague standing nearby with a collection of small plastic bags on the ground by her feet and called her over. 'We did find something that might interest you, though. Gareth found these in his pocket.'

Turpin frowned as the CSI handed over the bag, three yellow pills at the bottom.

'Ever seen something like this before?'

'I don't recognise it. You?'

Jan watched while her colleague turned the

bag in his hands then tilted it so it fell under the glare of the floodlight.

'No,' he said. 'Is it new?'

'We'll run some tests when we get them to the lab. It could take a while though,' said Jasper.

'I know.' Turpin sighed. 'Anything else?'

'We've bagged up a couple of receipts and a bus ticket for processing that we found scrunched up in his pocket,' said Gareth.

'What about a mobile phone?'

'Nothing yet.'

'All right, thanks. Jasper – can you let us have your report as soon as you can? You'll let us know if the weapon turns up?'

The CSI lead nodded. 'And I'll call you if we find anything else that might help you.'

'Thanks.' Turpin turned on his heel.

Jan stood for a moment, her gaze roaming over the blood stains that slicked the ground.

What had brought him here?

Where were his family?

Why would someone want to kill him?

Turpin nudged her with his elbow and jerked his chin towards the entrance to the alleyway.

'Come on.'

She nodded, her throat tight. 'Sarge.'

Following him back towards Market Place, her heartbeat thudding in her ears as loudly as the beat that still pounded from the fair's sound system, she wondered what had gone wrong in the youngster's life that had ended with him dying alone, here.

Ahead of her, Turpin waved over a police sergeant she recognised as a local, and brought him up to date with Jasper's findings.

'We'll head to the station now. Kennedy's already there setting up an incident room, so we'll assist with that and then go through what we know to date.' Turpin peered over the police sergeant's shoulder towards one of the ride operators and raised his voice. 'And will someone turn that bloody music off?'

CHAPTER FIVE

The distinct smell of burnt coffee beans and stale body odour smacked Jan in the face when she pushed open the door to the incident room half an hour later.

Neither she nor Turpin had brought their cars to the fair, preferring instead to walk rather than fight for a parking space given they both lived close to the town centre. By the time they had edged their way through the crowds leaving Ock Street via the cordons, refusing to comment to the nosier members of the public as to what had happened, she was desperate to reach her desk and make a start on what would be a long night.

Desks had been pushed away from the front of the room to make space for a clean whiteboard that would become the focus of every briefing until the new murder case was solved, and a frenetic energy hung in the air.

A low hum filled the incident room, the sounds of busy voices, busy telephones, busy computers. There was only a skeleton crew at this short notice, but everywhere she looked, there was activity.

As she ran her eyes over the gathered officers, she noticed others bearing evidence of their attendance at the fair.

A large teddy bear sat beside Police Sergeant Tom Wilcox, while the officer leaned close to his computer monitor, the pale glow from the screen illuminating his face as he worked.

The remnants of food wrappers, glitter-covered helium balloons and more scattered amongst the desks looked too cheerful, too bright for such a sombre atmosphere.

She checked her watch – half past eleven, over an hour since Turpin had phoned her with news of the boy's murder.

DI Kennedy's office door was shut, but she

could see him through the blinds at the window. Phone to his ear, head bowed, he ran a hand through his thin hair as he listened to the person at the other end.

'Here.'

She managed a smile as a mug of coffee was thrust at her. 'Thanks, Sarge. I'll get logged in to my computer, and then have a chat with Tom about how he's getting on setting up a new case in the HOLMES2 database so we can get our notes updated before tomorrow morning's briefing.'

'Okay, good. As soon as Kennedy's off the phone, he wants a word with me. After that, I'll give you a hand.'

Jan nodded, put the coffee next to her computer keyboard and signed in.

As her computer whirred to life, her gaze fell upon the framed photograph beside her phone, her twin boys grinning at the camera. Scott had snapped the picture during a two-week holiday in Devon that summer.

Her throat constricted, tears pricking at the corners of her eyes. She sniffed, wiped the tears away with the cuff of her sweatshirt, and straightened her shoulders.

The team would work all hours to find out who was responsible for the boy's murder, and she vowed to make sure she was there when an arrest was made.

She was working through a spate of emails that required delegation and action by others when Kennedy's office door was thrust open and he peered out into the room.

'Good, you're both here.' He beckoned to Turpin. 'Let's have a word. Jan – do you want to join us?'

'Guv.'

Snatching up her notebook and a fresh biro from her desk, she weaved through a forest of chairs towards the DI, nodding to Turpin as he stood at the threshold to the office to let her in first.

'Shut the door, Mark. Both of you – have a seat.' Kennedy gestured to the two visitor's chairs opposite his desk, and settled into his own, clasping his hands. 'Okay, first things first, how are things progressing at the scene?'

'Uniform are working with the security contractors employed by the council to take as many names and addresses of people leaving the fair as possible,' said Turpin. 'An ambulance crew confirmed the death, and the coroner's office sent out a van. Jasper has two teams working the crime scene from the Market Place end of the alleyway through to the exit behind the shops and through to Broad Street, with uniform coordinating from there. I've also spoken with the fair's manager and a council representative, guv. They're due to start dismantling the rides from midnight in time to re-open all routes through the town before rush hour tomorrow.'

Kennedy leaned back and rubbed his chin, a shadow speckling his jawline. 'And I have a feeling they'll protest if we say otherwise.'

'The boy was murdered away from the rides on Ock Street,' said Turpin, 'and we have contact details for all fair personnel. I think in the circumstances, we let them get on with it. Statements are being taken by uniform at the moment, and those will continue through the night while the rides are packed away. If they hear anything suspicious, we can make a decision then whether to hold back that person for further questioning.'

'I agree, but make sure no-one leaves without

giving a statement,' said Kennedy. 'Where are we with CCTV?'

'I walked the perimeter of Market Place and have a list of privately- and council-owned camera positions,' said Jan. 'There's also a bank ATM that should have a camera that we can request footage from. Uniform were conducting a walk-through of other streets leading away from the square and we'll put in the formal requests to the council first thing tomorrow morning.'

'Good. Well, I've spoken to the Chief Super – he'll arrange for us to receive additional administrative support from tomorrow afternoon, and I've also asked Caroline and Alex to come in tomorrow as well. They weren't rostered until Thursday, but…' Kennedy shrugged.

It was what it was.

Jan knew both of her colleagues would rearrange plans for their time off without complaint.

The DI drummed his fingers on the desk, then glanced at his watch. 'All right, I think that's enough for tonight. I'll send everyone home as soon as they've got themselves up to date out there. No point in having a room full of tired officers when we need to press on first thing. First thing tomorrow, can you two get yourselves over to the house of the woman who found the boy –

Clare Baxter, wasn't it? – and go through her statement before you come here? See if she recalls anything else that might help us.'

'Will do, guv,' said Turpin, pushing his chair back and stretching. 'Any news on when Gillian might fit in the post mortem this week?'

'I gave her a call before you got back. She's scheduled it for Friday morning, but said she'll bring it forward if her workload allows.' Kennedy held up his hands. 'There's a court case tomorrow, so that's taking precedence, I'm afraid.'

'See you in the morning, guv,' said Jan.

She traipsed after Turpin from the office, pausing at her desk as he stuffed his mobile phone back in his pocket. 'Do you want me to pick you up in the morning?'

'That would be good, thanks.' He shrugged on his coat. 'Can you make it about eight o'clock? I've got to go and get the girls from Lucy's, and it'll probably take them a couple of hours to calm down by the time I get them home tonight.'

'No problem.' She switched off her computer

and shouldered her bag, before phoning a local taxi company and following Turpin out of the door.

She couldn't wait to get home and see her two boys safe in their beds.

Safe from a killer who had stabbed a child, and left him to die alone.

CHAPTER SIX

Mark saw Jan into a taxi outside the police station, then flipped up his collar and shoved his hands in his pockets before setting off for the river.

The light rain had eased, leaving oil-streaked puddles in the gutters and an atmosphere that became more oppressive as he walked towards the abandoned fair.

He nodded to two uniformed constables who were walking towards him, their faces grim and shoulders slumped.

'Thanks for your help tonight,' he said as they drew nearer.

'Sarge,' said the shorter of the two.

No other conversation was necessary; they all bore the burden of the boy's death.

As their footsteps disappeared behind him, he picked up his pace.

The gravity wheel ride beside the double roundabouts stood silent, two of the fairground workers standing at its base while four more clambered around the metal structure and began the painstaking job of dismantling it in such a way that it could be set up again at its new location as quickly as safety allowed.

The two men stopped and stared at Mark as he passed, their faces shadowed by woollen hats pulled down low over their heads. A wisp of smoke escaped one man's lips before he turned away with a sneer, his attention returning to his colleagues working above.

He wondered how much money the ride operators had lost that night, then discarded the thought with the next eye blink. Money was irrelevant given the circumstances, and he had no doubt that the fairground's insurers would be receiving a phone call in the morning.

Holding up his warrant card to the security

guard who manned the remaining crowd control barriers blocking access to the street, Mark stepped around the metal gate and into Ock Street.

Street cleaners worked, heads bowed against a wind that frustrated their efforts as they hosed pavements and swept litter from crevices and shop steps. In a few hours, the road would be opened for the morning rush hour traffic and no sign of the past night's activities would remain.

The mile-long stretch of road gave him ample time to reflect upon the evening's events.

If he had been more attentive, if he had been closer to the alleyway, if he had—

Stop.

Side-stepping a pool of vomit the street cleaners hadn't yet reached, he wrinkled his nose at the pervading stench and then turned the corner into Bridge Street.

A fresh and welcome breeze buffeted against him as he passed the closed shops and takeaways, a large rat scurrying away as he drew closer to the bridge, a morsel clutched between its jaws.

He paused when he reached the arch of the bridge, resting his forearms on the stonework.

Upstream, a short string of boats was moored

in the distance. Far enough away from the traffic noise, far enough away for the owners to be cocooned from the outside world if they chose.

Setting off once more, a renewed energy in his stride, he cut through a gap next to a metal five-bar gate, switched on his phone's torch app and walked at a brisk pace towards a dark green narrowboat at the end of the row of vessels.

A warm glow shone beyond the closed curtains, and when he stepped onto the gunwale a light winked on above the cabin door.

The door opened before he could knock, and Lucy put her finger to her lips.

'They've been fast asleep for the past half an hour,' she said, her voice low. 'They wanted to stay up and wait for you, but I think exhaustion set in after they'd had supper and a hot drink.'

Mark wrapped his arms around her, and closed his eyes.

After a moment, she shifted and raised her gaze to his. 'Are you okay?'

'I will be.' He peered down as Hamish bounded over and sniffed at his shoes. 'I'll call a taxi – it's not fair on the girls to walk home at this time of night.'

Lucy squeezed his hand. 'Leave them here. Hamish, too. I'd imagine you're going to be out early in the morning, aren't you?'

He turned from her, took in the discarded paperback on top of a quilt thrown over one of the cabin seats, and frowned.

'Don't worry about me,' said Lucy. 'I'm comfortable enough there. It's where I usually sleep when I have friends stay.'

'I feel guilty imposing on you like this.'

'You're not. The girls are great.' She smiled. 'Although I might not say that tomorrow night if they keep kicking my arse at Monopoly.'

Mark smiled, some of the tension easing from his body at her words.

She was right, of course. He would be back in the incident room at daybreak, and likely there for a long time.

'They're not going back to school this week, are they?' Lucy continued. 'Not with Debbie away and half-term starting next week.'

'They've still got homework to hand in. They've been doing so well – Debbie'll shoot me if they get behind this late into the term.'

'Leave them here, Mark. I'll keep them occupied. We'll be fine.'

'Okay. Thank you.' He looked down at the small dog.

'Hamish can stay here too, don't worry.'

Mark pulled his keys from his pocket and wiggled one from the novelty ring Louise had bought him for Father's Day the previous year. He gave a shy smile as he handed it over. 'Just in case it gets too cramped here for all of you. I'll call in first thing tomorrow with a change of clothes for them, but if I've forgotten anything they can at least go around and get it.'

'How will you get in?'

'There's a spare hidden near the back door.'

Lucy plucked the key from his fingers. 'Can you bring Hamish's bowls and some food for him, too? Since he's been living with you I haven't stocked up on biscuits for him.'

'Will do.' He reached out and tilted her face towards his, kissing her. 'Thanks again. I don't know what I'd do without you.'

'I know.' She winked, then gave him a gentle shove. 'Now, go home and get some sleep. I think you're going to need it.'

CHAPTER SEVEN

Mark woke up to a chilly bedroom ten minutes before the alarm was due to go off and reached out for the bedside light.

He leaned across the bedside table for the glass of water he'd placed there in the early hours of the morning and drank half in three gulps before checking the time again, then switched off the alarm setting on his phone.

Seven o'clock. Six hours since he had left Lucy's boat.

The walk home had at least allowed him time to let his mind work through the events of the night, although it had given him no answers.

A new notification caught his attention, and he opened it to see a reply from Jan to the message he'd sent before crawling into bed.

She was picking him up in an hour.

Rubbing at eyelids that scratched at his vision and did nothing to erase the lack of sleep, he pushed back the covers with a mixture of dread and foreboding.

A hot shower did nothing to lift his mood – when a murder enquiry revolved around the death of a child, it lent a different dynamic to the investigation, especially when many of the officers rostered to work alongside him and Jan had families of their own.

His thoughts turned to his own daughters, a guilt seizing him that he had been left with no choice but to take up Lucy's offer to look after Anna and Louise overnight instead of spending the time with them.

The house felt empty without the girls and Hamish – ever since their arrival on Saturday, it had been filled with the sounds of a happy bedlam.

Now it seemed abandoned.

Fifteen minutes later, he was pulling the front

door closed when a silver hatchback car swung into the cul-de-sac and braked to a halt at the end of the garden path.

Jan climbed out and rested her arms on the roof as he approached. 'Morning, Sarge.'

'Thanks for picking me up.' He held up the bags. 'Do you mind if we stop at Lucy's boat first? They're staying with her today.'

'No problem.'

After putting the bags on the back seat, Mark opened the passenger door to the car, slid his seatbelt over his chest, and fought back a yawn as Jan twisted the key in the ignition.

'Don't,' she said. 'You'll start me off.'

'What time did you get to sleep last night?'

'Can't remember. I didn't sleep well, that's for sure.'

———

Twenty minutes later, he left Jan waiting for him in the council car park and hurried across the meadow to Lucy's boat.

A waft of smoke escaped the chimney in the roof, evidence that she was making full use of the wood-burning stove in the cabin at this time of year, and she opened the cabin door as he stepped on board.

'Morning.'

'Morning,' he said, handing her the bags. 'Sorry to turn up so early. We've got to head out and interview a potential witness. Everyone sleep okay?'

'Like logs. They're still in bed. I'm about to start doing bacon and eggs, so that should get them up and about.'

'You're an angel. Thank you.'

'No problem. I thought we'd take Hamish for a walk later – he hasn't been along the towpath for a while, and I know a place near Nuneham Courtenay where we can stop for a bite to eat if the weather holds.'

His shoulders relaxed a little. 'The fresh air will wear them out.'

'That's what I thought.'

Mark caught sight of the clock on the galley wall. 'Listen, I've got to go. I'll pick up fish and chips for all of us on my way home from work. Will you be all right to meet me back there with them?'

'Sounds good. I'll bring wine.'

When he reached the car, the hems of his suit trousers were wet and he adjusted the temperature controls in the car until a hot wind feathered his shoes.

He sighed. 'Okay, let's go and see if Clare Baxter can remember anything else from last night that can help us.'

Jan reached across to the footwell, rummaged in her bag, and handed him a foil package warm to the touch.

'While I'm driving, eat that. I'll bet you didn't have breakfast, and the mobile café over there was doing a two-for-one offer.'

CHAPTER EIGHT

Clare Baxter lived in a terraced cottage a few minutes north of Gozzard's Ford, a tiny hamlet that skirted the airfield north of the town.

According to the statement taken by uniform the night before, Clare had worked in the café for two years since her youngest child had started infant school. Her husband worked as a long-distance haulage driver and on days when he was home, she took on extra shifts to top up their savings.

Mark closed the email on his phone and climbed from the car, following Jan as she pushed through a wooden gate set into a low hedgerow.

Various children's toys lay around the small front lawn; a football softened through use, a single swing set rusting at the edges, and a trampoline that took up most of the space.

A thick-set man in his mid-thirties opened the front door after Jan knocked, introduced himself as Tim, and held out a giant paw of a hand upon being shown her warrant card.

'Thanks for coming around here instead of making her go to the police station,' he said. 'She was in a right state by the time she got home last night.'

He led the way through to a tiny kitchen at the rear of the property where they found Clare packing lunches into two backpacks and her young son and daughter sitting at a table in the corner.

She gave Mark and Jan a wan smile. 'Do you mind if we get these two off to school first?'

'Not at all,' said Mark. He turned to the children. 'How are you doing at school? Looking forward to the holidays next week?'

The boy lowered his gaze to the tiled floor and swung his feet, his face reddening, but his older sister nodded in earnest.

'We're going to visit Nanny,' she said, her voice clear.

'Oh, very nice – where does she live?'

The girl frowned for a moment before answering. 'Where Robin Hood lives.'

Mark smiled. 'Nottingham.'

He got a nod in response.

'We thought it would be good to get away for a bit,' said Tim. 'After last night, I just want to take Clare away. These two start half-term on Friday, so timing-wise—'

'Is that all right?' said his wife, frowning. 'I mean, will I be allowed to?'

'Just let us have a phone number and an address in case we have to clarify anything after we have a chat this morning,' said Mark, 'but it shouldn't be a problem.'

'Thanks,' said Tim. 'Okay, you two. Bags are packed. Give your mum a kiss.'

As her family left the kitchen, Clare's face turned wistful and she wrapped her arms around her waist.

'Do you want to sit down?' said Jan, pulling out her notebook.

The woman indicated they should take the

chairs the children had been sitting in, then dragged out a third from under the table and collapsed into it, her face growing paler by the minute.

'I keep trying to pretend nothing's wrong for their sake,' she said. 'We haven't said anything to them, but they can tell something's up this morning.'

'Children are incredibly perceptive, Mrs Baxter,' said Mark. 'But they seem keen to get to school.'

Voices sounded from the hallway, and then the front door slammed and a silence fell on the house. The clock above the microwave ticked away for a moment, and then the woman shook her head as if to clear her thoughts.

'Please, call me Clare.' She shuffled the seat forward and clasped her hands together on the table. 'What do you need to know?'

'Can you tell me what happened last night?' said Mark. 'Why were you working late?'

'Tim had a job up to Aberdeen and back that got cancelled – we need the money, he doesn't get so much work these days, and Angie who owns the café hadn't had a day off in over a week so I phoned up and offered to help out.' Clare threaded her fingers through a delicate silver chain around her neck. 'I went in at three o'clock – Angie decided to stay open late last night to see if she could make a bit of extra money with the fair being on and everything.'

'What time were you on your own from?'

'She left at seven. It wasn't that busy, to be honest – maybe one or two people in at a time, and so I told her to head off and that I'd close up. I don't have a key, but I'm due in later today so she gave me her spare and went home.'

'What time was it when you went out to the alley?'

'Just after ten. The café had been quiet since nine, so I'd spent the time mopping the floor and cleaning up ready for the morning.' Her hand dropped from the chain. 'I decided to take the bins out last thing.'

Mark remained silent, watching Clare's face as her eyes fell to the table and she bit her lip.

'I didn't see him at first,' she said. 'I suppose I was just concentrating on getting the rubbish out to the bins and then getting home. It wasn't until I'd thrown the bags in and closed the lid that I spotted him. I turned around and he was just – there. Slumped against the wall.'

She pushed back her chair and moved to the worktop, pulling sheets from a roll of kitchen towel and wiping her eyes. Scrunching up the towel in her hand, she turned and sniffed.

'Sorry. I keep seeing his face in my mind.' Clare blinked, and leaned against the worktop. 'It took me a few seconds to realise what was going on. I mean, you hear about this sort of thing happening in Oxford and bigger places, don't you? Not here. There was blood everywhere, smeared against the wall and all over the floor underneath him. When he didn't move, I panicked. I didn't know what to do. I knew I had to get help.'

Mark gave her a few moments to compose herself, then leaned forward. 'Had you ever seen him before?'

She shook her head. 'No.'

'Not in the café or perhaps at your children's school?'

'No, I think I would remember if I had. I-I can't get his face out of my mind.'

CHAPTER NINE

A sombre mood greeted Jan as she pushed open the door into the incident room and crossed over to her desk.

The volume of voices that accompanied the day-to-day work of policing the town and surrounding villages had disappeared while grim faces peered at computer screens.

Administrative staff rushed back and forth from the two printers set against a wall facing the whiteboard, distributing tasks and reports as new information became available and the detectives were delegated tasks through the HOLMES2 system.

A stack of papers tottered on top of a table in the middle of the room, and Jan realised as she passed that these were the official statements collated from people at the fair last night.

Uniformed officers would be tasked with contacting those who had provided information and obtaining signatures to formalise the process, and then it would be down to the rest of the investigating team to re-read through the results and try to find some answers.

She switched on her computer, running through the slew of voicemail messages that had been left on her desk phone in her absence, and had started to delegate some of her emails to colleagues when she sensed a presence at her elbow.

'How did it go this morning?'

Detective Constable Alex McClellan tucked his crumpled white shirt into his trousers, his face eager. He was the most junior member of the detectives that worked out of the Abingdon station, and Jan spent a lot of her time trying to decide whether to mother him or throttle him.

Not today.

Not with a dead child in the morgue in Oxford.

'Clare Baxter confirmed he wasn't moving when she found him,' she said. 'He'd already lost too much blood by then.'

Alex's shoulders dropped. 'I haven't had to work on a murder case involving a kid before. Will I have to go to the post mortem?'

'If it's assigned to you, yes.' She shoved her computer mouse away and spun her chair around to face him. 'How did the briefing go?'

'It didn't – Kennedy was asked to attend a meeting with the Chief Superintendent first thing, so he was planning to do it when you got back. I reckon—'

He broke off as the door burst open, and the detective inspector strode into the room.

Kennedy tugged at his tie as he approached Turpin's desk, nodded to Jan and Alex, and raised his voice.

'Five minutes, front of room everyone,' he said. 'Now that the Super is happy with his budget forecast for next year, he's asking for updates on this enquiry, so let's have something to report by the end of the day.'

His words were met with a murmur of grumbles from the administrative and uniformed staff, which he ignored. Instead, he rolled up his tie and placed it in his jacket pocket.

'From the look on your face, Mark, I'm guessing our witness didn't provide any further information about what went on last night?'

'No, guv – sorry.' Turpin's voice matched the frustration in his eyes. 'Apparently the victim was already dead by the time Clare Baxter found him.'

'Bugger.' Kennedy sighed, and jerked his chin towards the whiteboard. 'All right, it is what it is. Let's get this briefing underway and see what we've got to work with so far. Jasper has emailed over photographs from last night – Caroline, can you make sure the ones we discussed earlier are pinned up so I can refer to them?'

Detective Constable Caroline Roberts tucked a strand of blonde hair behind her ear as she scribbled a note to herself. 'Will do, guv.'

Jan watched as her tall colleague hurried away, then turned back to Turpin. 'If you need to leave at a reasonable time tonight to pick up the girls, I don't mind staying – Scott's going to collect the boys from school as usual and then they're off to see a football match in Oxford as a treat. Hopefully it'll take their minds off last night.'

Turpin snatched a biro from the pen pot between their desks and turned to a fresh page in his notebook before following her to where their colleagues were starting to gather. 'Did they ask any questions this morning?'

She glanced over her shoulder and gave him a rueful smile. 'Only whether the fair was back tonight so they could have another ride on the dodgems.'

She nodded her thanks as he gestured to the last remaining seat at the front of the throng, and he hovered beside Alex while Kennedy arranged his notes and provided an overview of the boy's death for the benefit of any staff members who were new to the investigation team.

'Right, let's get on with finding out what we can about our victim,' he said.

Stepping aside, he gestured to a photograph that Caroline had pinned in the centre of the whiteboard.

The dead boy.

Jan swallowed, and heard one of the administrative staff sniff at the back of the group.

The staff at the morgue had washed away the blood that had covered the boy's features. With his eyes closed, mouth slack, in death the boy could have looked as if he were asleep.

Movement on the other side of the room caught her attention, and she looked across in time to see Turpin stagger, his face pale.

She frowned as he caught her eye, but he shook his head, then crossed his arms over his chest and turned his attention to Kennedy as the DI began to speak once more.

'Thanks to those of you who worked into the early hours of this morning to assist Jasper's team to work around the crime scene and surrounding streets,' he said. 'To date, no weapon has been found, but as you can see from the map here, there are plenty of escape routes leading away from the town centre. I want an underwater search team tasked with working their way between the wharf on St Helen's Street and the Abbey Gardens as a starting point in case our killer decided to throw it into the river – Caroline, can you coordinate that and provide updates?'

The detective constable nodded, and bowed her head over her notebook.

'Next,' said Kennedy. 'No identification was found on our victim, but some items were found that will require following up – Tom, can you let us have an update on that, please?'

'The bus ticket was purchased at Didcot Parkway train station yesterday morning at five forty-five,' said the police sergeant. 'It looks like he paid cash for a bottle of water at the station, and then an energy drink in Abingdon in the afternoon.'

'Thanks. Okay, Alex – can you start collating CCTV and any private security camera footage from the train station and those shops so we can try to trace our victim's movements prior to his death? Have a word with the bus company, too.'

'Yes, guv.'

'And I'll need you to accompany Jan to the post mortem when we've got a date and time.'

'Okay.'

Jan could hear the reluctance in the junior detective's voice and caught Kennedy's eye before giving him a slight nod. The DI tended to seek out his team's weaknesses and do his best to alleviate them – it might seem cruel, but it worked.

'One final thing I need to mention, guv,' said Tom, and tapped a third photograph. 'Three yellow pills were found caught in the seam of the boy's jeans pocket. Two more were found in the road behind the shops on Stert Street, near a loading bay.'

'Drug deal gone wrong then?' called out a police constable. 'Did someone nick his stash?'

'Possibly,' said Kennedy. 'So we need to find out if he was the buyer or the seller. Does anyone recognise the branding on one side of the pills? It's a radioactive trefoil.'

A murmur of negative responses filled the air.

'All right – what about the colour? Is that significant?'

'Same colour as Oxford's football team strip,' said an administrative assistant, who then blushed.

'Good point.' Kennedy jotted down a note next to the photograph and re-capped the pen. 'At the present time, everything could be relevant, so I don't want anyone keeping ideas to themselves.'

'If those are a new type of drug we haven't

seen before, should we consider a new supplier in the area?' said Jan.

'The last thing we need is a turf war,' said Kennedy. 'Has Jasper given any indication when the test results might be in so we can find out what's in these?'

'He reckons it'll be next week at least,' said Caroline. 'They're sending the samples off to an independent contractor who already has a backlog.'

More grumbles.

'Follow up with Jasper on Friday afternoon to see if he's been given a better idea of that timeline,' said the DI, and gestured towards Tracy on the far side of the room. 'Can you update the system with that information as well?'

'Will do, guv.'

Kennedy glanced at his watch. 'All right, that will do for now. Unless there's a major breakthrough this afternoon, the next briefing will be tomorrow morning at eight o'clock sharp.'

As the group broke up and moved back to their desks, Jan wandered across to where Turpin stood, his face anxious.

'Are you okay?'

'Hang on a minute.' He held up his hand as Kennedy passed on his way to his office. 'Guv, can I have a word?'

'It'll have to be this afternoon, Mark – I've got a press conference at Kidlington to get to, and Sarah won't thank me if I'm late.'

Jan frowned as Turpin stepped in front of the DI, his tone urgent.

'Guv, I need to talk to you now.'

Kennedy raised his eyebrow. 'What is it?'

'I recognise him, guv. The boy. I know who he is.'

CHAPTER TEN

Kennedy pointed to the two visitor's chairs next to his desk.

'Sit.'

Mark waited while Jan lowered herself into the chair nearest the door as if she were already plotting her escape, and then took the seat beside her.

Kennedy swept paperwork and his diary to one side, then picked up his desk phone and told the media team he would be running fifteen minutes late. When he slammed it back into its cradle, the noise echoed off the plaster walls.

He exhaled, then turned to Jan. 'I'm including

you in this conversation to save Mark explaining himself twice.'

'Guv.'

Her voice was strained and she kept her eyes on the DI, her back ramrod straight although Mark noted the way she twisted her hands in her lap.

He cleared his throat, a tightness clawing at his chest as Kennedy's attention turned to him.

'Care to tell me why you didn't inform me of this last night?' said the DI. 'It would've saved us time, for a start.'

'Sorry, guv. I didn't make the connection when I first saw him. I haven't seen him in nearly three years. He must've been only nine or ten at the time. It was only seeing the photo with his face cleaned up that I recognised him. He's changed quite a bit.'

'Does this have anything to do with what happened to you in Swindon?'

'It might do, guv.'

The DI stepped around his desk and moved to the door, shutting it with such force that the window rattled. He pulled the blinds down and then sat.

'Explain. Who is the boy?'

'I only know his first name, guv. It's Matthew. He must be about fourteen years old now.'

'When did you last see him?'

'A few days before I was stabbed.'

'How was he related to that case?'

'We suspected at the time he was being groomed by the gang as part of an ongoing county lines operation,' said Mark. 'We'd seen him hanging around with some of the people who were known buyers while we were trying to establish how the gang was networking its way into Swindon. None of the youngsters used to distribute the drugs was old enough to drive, so based on the rail network into the town, we were working on the basis of tracing the deals back to their origin. London was an obvious choice, as were Bristol and Reading.'

'Was Matthew a buyer or a seller?'

'At first, we thought he was a local but we couldn't locate where he was staying or who his family was. That then led us to believe he was tagging along with one of the other sellers and travelling in from their base town to learn from him.'

'So what the hell is he doing here?' said Kennedy.

'I don't know,' said Mark. 'He disappeared from sight a few days before I was attacked. A couple of others did, too – the older ones.'

Kennedy raised an eyebrow. 'That sounds to me like they caught wind of your operation to infiltrate the gang by arresting the dealers.'

Mark swallowed, ignoring the goosebumps that pricked his forearms. 'I thought that at the time.'

The DI leaned back in his chair and drummed his fingers on the desk for a moment, then turned to Jan.

'I'm going to ask you to keep what we're about to discuss in the strictest confidence unless and until we have more information to link this boy's murder to what happened to Mark, due to the fact it still forms part of an ongoing investigation by Wiltshire police, is that clear?'

'Yes, guv.'

He nodded, then turned his attention back to Mark. 'Why did the operation go ahead when it did?'

'We'd always assumed that the county lines

operation was coming *into* Swindon and targeting users there. I wondered if that wasn't the case. Before our informant died, he told me the operation was *starting* in Swindon. The organisers were looking to expand beyond the Wiltshire border, establishing their own county lines operation. If they concentrated on towns like this and Wallingford – all of those are easily accessible by bus from Didcot station, and it alleviates the risk of any cars that are being used to transport large amounts of drugs being picked up by the Automated Number Plate Recognition cameras. There are fewer CCTV cameras in operation at bus stops than train stations, so it'd be easier for them. I ran my theory past my DI and he escalated it. We were worried that if the gang did carry out that expansion it'd be even more difficult to rein it in and arrest the ones running it – they'd simply fade into the background, set up a legitimate business in Swindon as a front to protect themselves, and deny any involvement.'

Kennedy's eyes narrowed. 'And then your informant got himself killed, and you nearly joined him. So tell me – because there's nothing on your file – what happened to the man who stabbed you, and then tried to throttle you?'

Mark heard the frustration in the DI's voice, and realised he had miscalculated.

By trying to create distance between his history and his new life, he had omitted vital information that could have given fair warning to his colleagues that an old enemy still had some scores to settle with him.

He should have trusted them.

He should have told them all this a year ago.

He took a deep breath. 'He died before the case came to court.' He tried to ignore the burning sensation at the back of his throat. He was talking too much, and his damaged larynx was starting to protest. 'He was being held on remand in prison – he accidentally fell down the stairs one morning on his way to the gym and broke his neck, although I'm not so sure about the accident part.'

'And you think he was killed so he couldn't talk about what happened?'

'It would make sense – he stabs the informant, realises that the man hasn't died before speaking to me, and then tries to silence me as well. Makes you wonder who he was working for, because to attack a police officer like that is a hell of a risk to take. When it didn't go according to plan, someone decided to make sure he didn't tell anyone who he worked for in the hope of making a deal for a reduced sentence.'

'You didn't want to investigate his death yourself?'

'I didn't have a choice. I was in hospital, and then physiotherapy. After that, I was named as a potential witness for the prosecution if the gang leaders were ever charged. I couldn't go anywhere near the case.'

Kennedy glared at him. 'Cut the bullshit, Mark. Why did you ask to be transferred here? Why not go back to work in Swindon? Your senior officers would've given you a desk job given your qualifications and experience until the case went to court.'

'I was going to.' Mark dropped his gaze to his lap and blinked. 'That's what I wanted to do. I wanted to find out who was responsible – who was at the top – and help in any way I could.'

The DI said nothing, and waited.

'Look, it might've been me being paranoid – I don't have any evidence – but Louise, my eldest daughter came home from school one afternoon. It was a Friday – about six weeks after I'd left hospital. She looked scared, and when I asked her what was wrong, she said that there had been a blue car following her and Anna every time they walked out of the school gates at four o'clock that week. She'd see it parked outside the school, and then she'd take a shortcut through an alleyway that led through a housing estate. By the time she reached the main road again, she thought she'd lost it but then by the time she turned into our street, it'd be tailing her again.'

He shuffled in his seat to see Jan staring at him, a shocked expression on her face.

Dammit, he should have told her this.

All of it.

'As soon as Louise told us, I reported it to my senior officer and Debbie and I put our own security measures in place. I drove the girls to school and back every day, we had the locks changed on the house and new ones installed on all the windows as well as security lights above the front and back doors.' He sighed. 'Neither of us could sleep, and Debbie quite rightly blamed me. I brought it on my family. I put them in danger. That's when I put in my request to transfer. I hoped that if I moved here, whoever was running the gang would consider the threat removed and leave Debbie and the girls alone.'

'And instead, you ended up transferring right into the place where they were planning to infiltrate by the sounds of it,' said Kennedy through gritted teeth. 'And now we have a young boy dead, too. Which brings us full circle – why kill him?'

'I don't know, guv.'

Kennedy ran a hand over weary eyes as his desk phone rang, and answered it with a curt 'What?' Then: 'I'm on my way.'

He dropped the receiver back in its cradle and wagged his finger at Mark. 'This isn't the bloody secret service, Turpin. You should have told me all of this when you turned up here. Now I have to decide how much of this information I can divulge to my team out there without compromising what your colleagues are doing in Swindon.'

'Sorry, guv. I thought it was all on file.'

'Get out.'

Mark could feel his face burning and pushed

back his chair before crossing to the door and opening it for Jan.

'You should've told me,' she hissed under her breath.

She brushed past him without making eye contact, then crossed to her desk, picked up her bag, and stomped from the room.

CHAPTER ELEVEN

Mark pushed his key into the lock and walked into a house oozing warmth and noise.

Balancing the portions of fish and chips in one hand and using his chin to keep the pile steady while he tried to stop Hamish running outside, he shut the door and turned to see Lucy leaning against the doorframe into the living room, a smile dimpling her cheeks.

Some of the tension left his shoulders as she gave him a quick kiss, and then Louise and Anna burst into the hallway.

'Dad, Lucy took us to her studio this afternoon so we could do some painting—'

THE LOST BOY 83

'I caught a fish this morning, Dad!'

He hugged them both and passed the fish and chip packages to Louise. 'Sounds like you've had a busy day. Can you sort out trays, plates and cutlery while Lucy and I have a chat?'

He shook his head as their voices carried from the kitchen, Louise barking instructions at her younger sister amongst the clatter of crockery while the sound of Hamish's claws on the tiles clacked back and forth as he followed the aromas being unleashed. 'I hope they haven't worn you out.'

Lucy waited until he'd hung his coat on the newel post at the bottom of the stairs, then followed him into the living room and muted the television. 'They've been absolutely fine. You, on the other hand, look shattered.'

Mark ran a hand over his hair and sank onto the sofa. 'I knew the boy who was killed last night.'

Lucy dropped beside him and leaned forward, her gaze on the open door. 'How?'

'He was involved with the gang my team were trying to infiltrate back in Swindon.'

'What was he doing here?'

'I don't know.'

'Shit, Mark.'

'Ta-daaa!'

Anna appeared at the door, and wandered across to where he sat.

'Thank you, gorgeous,' he said, and winked. 'Beer, too? Blimey, I *am* a lucky man.'

'Louise said you'd probably want a glass of wine, but you looked like you needed beer.'

'Did I? Well, I might have a glass of wine after dinner, but this is perfect for now.'

Anna grinned then raced away, narrowly colliding with her sister who was carrying in an identical tray for Lucy.

'Thanks again for today,' she said. 'We had a lot of fun.'

'Oh, you're welcome,' said Lucy. 'I enjoyed it, too.'

Moments later, both girls had settled into the armchairs and were tucking into their food, bickering over who had the larger portion of fish while a reality TV show played out silently in the background.

Mark let the voices wash over him, clutching on to the sense of peace for a while.

He had thought about phoning Jan while he was waiting for his food order to be cooked, and stood with his thumb hovering over her name while he debated. In the end, he had put his mobile back in his pocket and watched the headlights from passing traffic swoop past the fish and chip shop, gritting his teeth at the normality that had returned to the world beyond the glass panes.

They would still have to interview the café owner in the morning, and he wondered whether Jan would collect him from his house as planned or whether he would have to walk.

'Finished, Dad?'

He blinked, then forced a smile on his face.

Louise was standing in front of him, a worried expression in her eyes.

'Sorry, love – miles away there. Thanks.'

He lifted his tray for her and watched as she and Anna traipsed back to the kitchen, the argument turning to who would wash up and whose turn it was to dry.

The sounds of voices paused for a moment, and then Anna returned, two glasses of red in her hands.

'Thank you,' said Lucy. 'Are you two all right out there?'

'Yes.' Anna turned, then paused in the middle of the room and glanced over her shoulder. 'I'm better at washing up, whatever she says. She uses too much soap.'

Mark laughed as she headed off, and then Hamish heard the sound of plates being scraped clean of food remnants and tore from the room, his tail in the air.

'Is that true, about the soap?' said Lucy.

'You'd better have shares in washing-up liquid.'

She reached out for his hand. 'What you were saying about knowing the boy? Does this have anything to do with you moving here from Swindon?'

'Yes.'

'Are the girls in danger?'

His stomach flipped. 'I don't know.'

'Are you in danger?'

Mark ran his thumb over the back of her hand. 'I don't think so.'

'Let them stay with me a bit longer.'

His head snapped up to be met with an intense

gaze. 'Are you a mind reader? I was going to ask if you'd mind—'

'Of course I don't mind. At least then you won't have to worry about anything happening to them here if this is all related to your old case. I borrowed one of my neighbour's cars to get here. They can bring a bag each – enough to last until Sunday night, say.'

'You're sure you don't mind?'

She reached out and squeezed his hand. 'What are you going to be doing for the next few days at least? Chasing leads, working long hours. The girls will be here alone, and bored. I haven't got another exhibition until next month and I can move some of my stuff from the boat to my studio to make a bit of extra room while they're with me.'

Louise and Anna returned, giggling.

'Hamish burped,' said Anna.

'I told her she gave him too much at once.' Louise rolled her eyes. 'You've got to be careful with dogs. They can get sick if they have the wrong food.'

'That's a good point,' said Lucy, her tone light. 'Hey – how do you two fancy staying with me for a bit longer while your dad works on this new case of his?'

Anna's eyes opened wide, her jaw dropping. 'Really?'

'Oh-my-God-are-you-kidding-me-that's-so—' Louise looked from Lucy to Mark, then back. 'Really?'

Mark shot Lucy a mock glare, then turned back to the girls. 'Until Sunday, *but* you'd better be on your best behaviour – and you can only take what you can pack into one bag each.'

He took a sip of wine while the girls' footsteps thundered up the stairs, then put his glass down and reached for his wallet. 'I'll give you some cash to help out with food and the like. Those two will eat you out of house and home, and—'

'I'm not taking your money,' said Lucy. She smiled. 'Trust me, I'll enjoy having the company. Louise said they've both been given assignments to do over this week, so they can do those in the mornings while I'm pottering around, and then I'll take them out in the afternoons. We'll be fine.'

Hamish whined at Mark's feet, and he sighed.

'Don't tell me. You want to go, too.'

CHAPTER TWELVE

The next morning, Mark hovered at the kerb and turned his back to the street as he checked his text messages.

A fresh breeze nipped at his earlobes and he pulled up his collar, wishing he had remembered to pluck his woollen hat from the coat rack next to the front door.

A grey sky threatened more rain, darkening his mood further.

The night had brought its share of troubled dreams, thoughts that made him lie awake, staring at the whorls in the ceiling while he worried.

Worried that he should have done more for

Matthew when he'd first spotted the kid three years ago.

Worried that if he had been a few seconds quicker, he might have saved his life.

He resisted the urge to check his watch – the time would show the same as the one on his phone, and there were still minutes to go. Still—

Perhaps she wasn't coming.

Perhaps he should start walking.

He lowered his phone as a car drove into the cul-de-sac, and spotted Jan at the wheel as she passed by, her jaw set, a thunderous expression in her eyes.

'Shit.'

The car rolled to a standstill beside him, and he opened the door.

'Morning.'

'Morning, Sarge.'

Jan's gaze remained on his neighbour's house in front of the car while he got in, and then the back of his head hit the seat as she pulled away.

A stony silence filled the car as she shoved the car into gear and pushed her way into the traffic inching along the Radley Road.

Mark shuffled in his seat until he faced her.

'Look, I'm sorry about what happened yesterday. With Kennedy, I mean. And I should've told you about what happened to me. All of it. I realise that now.'

Jan tapped her fingers on the steering wheel as the car in front inched forward before braking once more.

The clock on the dashboard flickered to the next minute.

'No more secrets, Sarge,' she said. 'Not if we're meant to trust each other.'

'Deal. I'm sorry. I never thought anything like this would happen. I hoped it was all behind me.'

'Apology accepted.'

His stomach rumbled, and he lowered his gaze to her open handbag in the footwell next to him.

No savoury aromas to tease his senses.

No foil-wrapped packages.

No free breakfast this morning.

'Guess I'm not forgiven.'

Her mouth twitched. 'Not yet.'

———

While Jan drove off to find a parking space in the multi-storey car park, Mark lingered under the concrete pedestrian footbridge leading to the library and tried to ignore the stench coming from the public toilets opposite.

A steady stream of people headed through the doors of the doctor's surgery behind him as he peered up at the cameras fixed to the topmost level of the car park. The lenses pointed left and right along Charter Street, and as he ran his gaze over the angles, he noticed more cameras on the wall of the library beside the surgery as well.

Surely one of them would have recorded Matthew's attacker fleeing the scene?

Perhaps they would show footage of Matthew himself, either moving towards the alleyway or away from whoever stabbed him?

The doorway opposite swung open and Jan appeared, pushing her hair out of the way while she crossed the road to join him.

'Bloody hell, this street is like a wind tunnel this morning,' she said, then followed his gaze. 'CCTV?'

'Plenty of it. Uniform are going to have their hands full. It'll be worthwhile taking some of the recordings off them and splitting it between us, Caroline and Alex, I reckon.'

'Leave the outer perimeter to uniform, you mean?'

'That's what I'm thinking. What time does the café open this morning?' he said, as they began to walk towards Queen Street.

'Six-thirty.'

'That early?'

'The owner – Angie Edwards – told me she needs to. Any later, and she'll lose trade to competitors. There are a lot of places for people to choose from around here.'

'No wonder Clare said she was grateful for the help. What do we know about Angie?'

Jan paused to let a red van pass by, and then hurried across the road and into Queen Street.

'Fifty-five years old, been running the place for the past six years. She's active with the local Chamber of Commerce and various other committees in town. No kids, divorced, and, from the statements uniform have gleaned from her other staff members, well respected.'

Mark moved out of the way of a delivery lorry manoeuvring away from the rear doors of one of the stores to his right and took in the bright yellow bins placed beside the brick wall of another building. 'Jasper phoned last night when they completed their search. No murder weapon.'

'Dammit. So, uniform will have to widen the search,' said Jan.

'What day are the council street collections around here?'

'The commercial ones are done tomorrow,' said Jan. 'I overheard Kennedy telling Alex yesterday to phone them and tell them to postpone until the search is complete.'

'That'll please residents.'

'Tough.'

He heard the break in her voice, the ragged edge of emotion, but said nothing.

He shared the sentiment.

At the end of Queen Street, nearest the rear entrance to the alleyway, a pair of plain white vans were parked while six members of Jasper's team wound the last remnants of crime scene tape away from shuttered delivery docks and bins.

Mark nodded to one of them as they passed.

A shiver ran across his shoulders when he and

Jan approached the back entrance to the alleyway, and he stopped.

'Sarge?'

He shook his head. 'If I'd been here sooner—'

'Mark.'

The sharpness of her tone caught him by surprise and he turned to face her.

'Don't,' she said. 'If he bled out that quickly, there was nothing you could have done for him. Nothing anyone could have done for him.'

'I know. Doesn't help though.' He managed a small smile, just enough to let her know he appreciated her concern.

'Come on.'

She didn't wait for him, but strode along the alleyway – although he noticed she kept to the left-hand side, away from where Matthew had been found, skirting close to the bins to avoid where the boy had lain.

Mark glanced at the wall and ground as they passed.

Someone had hosed down the area, and the distinct stench of bleach assaulted his nostrils, burning the back of his throat.

No doubt the council had surged into action as

soon as Jasper's team handed over the site, conscious of eliminating any traces of the boy's death before someone shared the squalid details on social media.

He coughed as they entered Market Place and then followed Jan into the café.

As was the case with many shops around the cobbled square and outlying lanes, space was at a premium – the right-hand wall was lined with open chiller cabinets containing soft drinks and pre-packaged snacks while three sets of tables and chairs took up the left-hand side. An older woman stood next to a cash register alongside a counter displaying freshly baked pies, sausage rolls and other pastries while voices carried from the rear of the café beyond an array of stainless steel appliances.

The aromatic sweetness of cakes mingled with the bitterness of the coffee beans, and Mark's mouth watered.

He reached into his pocket for his wallet as they reached the front of the short queue and ordered two coffees.

'You the police?' the woman said as she took

their order and turned to a coffee machine behind the till.

'Yes. Angie Edwards?'

'That's me,' she said over her shoulder. 'I presume you want a word?'

'Please.'

'Hang on.' She raised her voice and called to the back of the café. 'Can someone come out here and serve?'

She swiped Mark's card, rang the order into the till and gestured to the table nearest the window. 'Over here then.'

While Jan wedged herself into the seat in the corner, Angie wiped the table before shoving the cloth into a pocket on the front of her apron and then sat opposite Mark and gazed out of the window.

'Look at them all. Not a care in the world,' she said, a melancholy filling her voice. She shook her head, and then refocused on the two detectives before her. 'Have you spoken to Clare this morning? The poor woman's distraught.'

'Briefly,' said Mark. 'How long has she worked for you?'

'Just over two years. She was looking for

something part-time once her little boy started infant school and saw the advert I'd put in the window.'

'How many people do you employ?'

'Just her and the two with me today. All of them are part-time but we muddle along.'

Mark reached into his pocket for a copy of the photograph from the mortuary. He kept his hand over it for a moment. 'I'd like to show you a picture of the boy who was found in the alley last night. Is that all right?'

Angie nodded. 'Go on.'

He saw her take a deep breath and square her shoulders as he flipped over the image, shock reaching her eyes.

'Have you seen him before?'

'I'm not sure.'

'We think he's from Swindon way. Not local, but he might've turned up sometime in the last few weeks or days.'

'How old is he?'

'Fourteen, I think.'

'The poor lad.' Angie shifted in her seat and looked over to where her two staff members were serving the last in a steady string of customers. 'Let me ask them.'

She picked up the photograph and headed towards the till, nodding to a customer who eyed Mark and Jan with interest before hurrying through the door.

Jan tapped the end of her pen on her notebook and sipped her coffee. 'Do you want to have a word with anyone else in the square after this?'

'Only the food places to start off with,' he said. 'I reckon he'd have been into one of these within the past week – the cheaper ones like this, though.'

'What about the fast food place down by the motel?'

'That, too. If anything, we can try to narrow down what his movements were. At least we'll be able to check their security camera footage as well.'

'Detective Turpin?' Angie approached the table with another woman. 'This is Yvonne – she's been working with me for the past six months. She says she recognises the boy.'

'Well, I think I might.' The woman shot Angie

a sideways glance, and twisted her hands in the folds of her apron.

'Where did you see him?' said Mark.

Angie pulled out a seat and ushered Yvonne into it before greeting a woman in a business suit who hurried through the door.

Yvonne watched them move to the till together, then turned her attention back to the two detectives.

'Yesterday, about mid-morning, I think.'

'Was he on his own?'

'As far as I could tell. He bought one of the energy drinks from the fridge and a sausage roll – they're the cheapest hot food in the cabinet – and then stood out there to eat it. I didn't see anyone with him.'

'Did he say anything?'

'No. I thought he was a bit young to be out and about to be honest, what with the schools not breaking up until the end of the week, but he didn't cause any trouble and paid up.'

'Did you see where he went after he left here?'

'No, sorry – I had to serve a customer, and I suppose I sort of forgot all about him until… oh, dear.' The woman blinked. 'I have two grandsons about the same age.'

Five minutes later, having left business cards with Angie and her staff in case they could think of anything else to help with the investigation, Mark and Jan walked the perimeter of the square while they finished their coffees.

'We ought to go over to Didcot,' he said. 'Travelling by train from Swindon would've been Matthew's quicker option if he was travelling alone. I'll give the incident room a call on our way and find out if anyone's spoken to the duty staff this morning yet. It'll be a good idea to get onto someone at British Transport Police as well to see if there's any footage of him on the platforms or leaving trains coming into Parkway.'

CHAPTER THIRTEEN

Jan reversed the car into a space outside the railway station entrance and squinted against a breeze that spun dead leaves and litter into the air as she climbed out.

The blast of a horn carried from the station, and then a train pulled away from the platform, gathering speed as it headed out into the Oxfordshire countryside.

She locked the vehicle and fell into step beside Turpin as he stalked across the asphalt and around the back of a teal-coloured double decker bus that idled at the kerb, a grim determination in his stride.

Entering the ticket office, Jan cast her gaze over the tiled floor, its surface worn and uneven from the hundreds of people who passed across it every day. A member of staff pushed a mop back and forth, her eyes widening as Turpin approached and held out his warrant card.

'We need to speak to the station manager,' he said.

'I'll have to radio her. I think she's out whistling trains on platform four at the moment.'

'Thanks.'

The woman slid the cleaning bucket across the tiles and propped up a yellow health and safety sign before standing the mop in the corner of the ticket office, and then disappeared through a security door. She appeared moments later behind a man serving at the ticket window who watched the two detectives with interest before turning to a computer, his eyes darting between his work and Jan.

After a moment the woman returned, joining her colleague at the thick glass partition. Her voice squawked through the microphone.

'Sheila says if you head over to the platform, she can speak to you now. You'll just have to put up with her getting interrupted by trains. The next one's due in at quarter past. The stairs are that way.'

She pointed to a sign leading off in the direction of a subway path.

'Thanks.' Turpin threw a wave over his shoulder and headed towards the underpass.

The pungent stench of disinfectant greeted Jan as she followed him, and she put her hand over her nose and mouth to ward off the worst.

In the distance, a trembling began in the earth beyond the concrete and steel foundations of the station. She raised her gaze as a rumbling grew closer, then the roar of a train's wheels shot overhead before braking to a standstill. She swallowed, then brushed past Turpin, the idea of several tons of metal crashing through the ceiling raising goose bumps on her skin. When she reached the base of the steps leading up to platform four, she paused to let her colleague catch up.

'Not good with being underground?' he said.

She wrinkled her nose. 'Not when there's no fresh air.'

Climbing the steps, she spotted the station

manager standing beside a metal bench seat, her rotund figure bundled up within a green three-quarter length coat to offset the wind that buffeted the open space.

Hair tied back in an efficient bun, she held out a gloved hand as they approached. 'Sheila Cook. I'm the station manager.'

Jan waited while Turpin provided the introductions, and then paused while the train two platforms across pulled out from the station.

Turning back to the woman as the train disappeared into the distance, he waited until Jan had her notebook and pen ready.

'We're investigating the murder of a young boy at the fair in Abingdon on Monday night, and believe he arrived here earlier that morning,' he said. 'Were you on duty then?'

Sheila nodded. 'Yes, I was. This is my last rostered day on.'

'What time do you start in the morning?'

'I get here for four o'clock, along with a few of the others. As soon as that first train comes in on its way to Paddington, it's non-stop around here.'

Turpin extracted a photograph of Matthew from his pocket and handed it over.

'We're working with our colleagues in the CCTV control room at Abingdon to see if we can spot him on camera, but do you recall seeing him on Monday morning? A bus ticket was found in his pocket, and he purchased that here at five forty-five. We think he travelled from Swindon.'

The station manager bit her lip. 'If he came from Swindon, then he would've arrived on platform two. I was splitting my time between there and here – I don't remember him, but he's young. I'm sure I would've wondered what he was doing at that time of the morning if I had seen him. The problem is, when that train came in from Swindon, there's one over here heading back the other way that blocks my view. I can't see who's on the platform from here.'

Jan peered over Turpin's shoulder to the platform Sheila pointed out. 'Are the waiting rooms open at that time of the day?'

'Absolutely, especially this time of year,' said Sheila. 'Some customers use the vending machines to get a coffee while they're waiting rather than buy one on the train – it's cheaper, you see.'

'Who else was working that platform on Monday morning?'

'Doug Jones, but he's off today – he only works part-time.'

'What about the café out near the ticket office?' said Turpin. 'What time does that open?'

'You say he bought a bus ticket at five forty-five?'

'Yes. We're working on the theory that he got the next bus into Abingdon.'

'They won't be able to help you, then – they don't open until six o'clock.'

'Is that covered by the same CCTV system as the rest of the station, or does the franchise have its own security in place?'

'It's the same system.'

'What about later on that morning?' said Jan. 'Do you recall anyone asking questions about a boy? Perhaps concerned that he might be travelling on his own?'

Sheila shook her head. 'Not that I recall. Mind you, my shift ends at twelve o'clock.'

'Can you give us a list of who else was

working that shift?' said Turpin. 'And a note of who was working the rest of the day?'

'That shouldn't be a problem. It'll have to get cleared by head office first, though.' Sheila handed back the photograph and took his business card before reciting her mobile phone number to Jan. 'I heard about the murder. I've got a daughter coming up to his age. If you need anything else, make sure you call me.'

'We will,' said Turpin. 'Thanks.'

As they made their way along the underpass, Turpin pulled out his phone.

'Well, at least we've got a contact here,' he said. 'And we know Matthew didn't loiter once he arrived. Good thinking about the possibility whoever followed Matthew came by train as well.'

'Perhaps he was travelling with someone,' said Jan. 'I mean, we've assumed until now that he was alone when he got here. What if he wasn't? What if he gave someone the slip?'

Turpin raised an eyebrow. 'Then maybe we've got them on camera, too.'

He waved for her to go on ahead as his call was answered.

She wandered across to the car and unlocked it, leaning against the door while she watched Turpin pace back and forth on the concourse.

After a few moments, he put his phone away and jogged over to join her.

'Tom's heading upstairs to the control room now – he'll ask them to add a review of the station CCTV footage to their task list in order to confirm Matthew's movements prior to getting the bus. He'll get them to look out for anyone who seems as if they were travelling with him, too.'

'We could've done that from the station, Sarge. Saved a trip over here.'

His shoulders slumped. 'I know. At least out here, I feel like I'm doing something useful though. At least it feels like I'm trying to find whoever did this to him. I couldn't save him in that alleyway. I've got to make it up to him somehow.'

Jan tossed the keys from hand to hand, squinting against the wind that whipped at her hair. 'What do you want to do now?'

'Let's head back, but take the same route that bus would've done on Monday morning. If anything, it'll give us a sense of where else

Matthew might've gone before ending up in that alley.'

Minutes later, Jan was guiding the car through the villages of Steventon and Drayton, her gaze sweeping the busy street that wound towards Abingdon as they passed.

'I can't imagine he'd have bothered stopping here, Sarge,' she said. 'Nothing to do.'

He bumped his fist on the door upholstery, then pulled out his notebook. 'I'll get uniform to call on anyone they can identify with a previous history of drugs use in the area. It's not much, but it'll at least allow us to rule out whether he was supplying to someone here. They're going to have to do the same with all known addicts in town anyway. Kennedy just hasn't given them the good news yet.'

'Okay.' Jan shifted gear as the traffic began to build up entering Abingdon, and pointed out a bus stop to their left. 'That's the last one on the Drayton Road he could've used. There are two more heading into the town centre, and the last one is near Market Place.'

He looked up from his notebook as she slowed the car and held up his hand. 'Wait – go left here.'

Jan flicked the indicator stalk, but not in time to avoid an angry honk from the vehicle behind them. She held up a hand over her shoulder to thank the driver, and glanced over to Turpin. 'The bus route goes right into Ock Street, not left. The next stop is Victoria Road.'

'I know, but the fast food restaurant is this way, opposite the police station. Matthew arrived first thing in the morning. He didn't stop to buy anything to eat at the convenience store at the train station, and the café there wasn't open at that time of the morning.'

'So, you think he got off the bus at the next stop, then doubled back to the fast food place?'

'They open at five o'clock every morning, don't they?' Turpin loosened his seat belt as she turned into the restaurant car park. 'Somehow we have to trace Matthew's movements, and if he had a bit of cash to get by then he might have been like one of our kids. Permanently hungry.'

CHAPTER FOURTEEN

Jan wrinkled her nose at the cloying stench of oil, grease and sugar that assaulted her when she opened the door into the fast food restaurant.

A bright yellow sign had been propped up on the tiled floor, warning of cleaning in progress but as she cast her gaze over the detritus of discarded wrappers and drink cartons strewn across the tables she passed, she wondered if the pronouncement was overambitious.

She raised her hand in greeting to a pair of police constables she recognised sitting at stools next to the window, the radio between them emitting a loud squawk before one of them reached out to turn down the volume.

A woman at a table with two toddlers glared at the back of one of the officers, and Jan sighed.

Many people joked about the preponderance of police personnel who frequented this and other fast food places in the area, but failed to realise that the police station didn't have a canteen or any of the comforts afforded to most modern offices.

There were only so many days you could live on toasted sandwiches – and that was if you were on duty in town. Anyone who was on call-out to the outlying villages was left to their own devices.

A group of six men and women moved behind the serving counter in a blur of panicked energy, all in their late teens or early twenties, while an older woman wearing a headset barked orders into a microphone, simultaneously peering out of the drive-through window. She swiped a customer's debit card with an exasperated flick of her wrist before turning her attention back to her staff.

The slurp and roar of a soft drinks machine fought with the racket of a toddler's scream from the play area, and Jan caught the look on Turpin's face.

'This is bedlam,' she said. 'Now I remember why I refuse to bring the kids here.'

She stepped aside to let an elderly man pass, a plastic tray laden with steaming pancakes and two coffee cups that slopped their contents under his shaking hands.

'Can I give you a hand with that?' she said.

'No.' His eyes blazed with indignation before he shuffled away.

Jan watched him reach a table off to one side, arranging a handful of paper sugar sachets in front of a woman with a perpetual scowl, and then turned her attention back to the counter.

Only one person remained waiting for their food order, and the window out to the drive-through was deserted.

'Now,' said Turpin under his breath, and launched himself towards the woman wearing the headset. 'Excuse me.'

She lifted her chin as they approached, a hand on her hip. 'Yes?'

Jan held out her warrant card. 'Detective Constable West, and this is my colleague Detective Sergeant Turpin. Can we speak to the manager, please?'

'I'm the duty manager. Beverley Swain.' The woman reached up and adjusted her short ponytail, rearranging a hair grip behind her ear.

'We need to take a look at your security camera footage. Is there somewhere we could talk? Perhaps somewhere a bit quieter?'

'You're joking.' The woman huffed out a laugh. 'The breakfast roster doesn't end until half ten.'

Jan checked her watch.

Forty minutes.

'This can't wait,' she said.

'Hang on. Billy!'

Jan's gaze swept the food preparation area behind the counter as the woman's voice rang out, and saw a lanky lad with bad acne sauntering towards them from the direction of the chip fryers.

'What's up, Bev?'

'I'll be in the office. Call me if it's urgent, and get Daisy out here to clean the tables.' The woman handed over the headset before beckoning to Jan and Turpin. 'Come on. I reckon we've got fifteen minutes before all hell breaks loose out here.'

Leading the way past the toilets, Beverley

swiped her security card across a panel beside a door marked "staff only", then opened an inner door and stepped to one side. 'In here.'

Jan's eyes found the row of six small screens behind a chipped flat-pack style desk as the manager joined them.

'How long do you keep the recordings for?' she said.

'Forever, as far as I know. It uploads to a central server. Why?'

Turpin reached into his jacket pocket and pulled out the photograph of Matthew. 'We're trying to find out if he came in here on Monday – or perhaps over the weekend. Do you recognise him?'

The woman's eyes widened. 'Is he the kid I heard got killed at the fair?'

'Did you see him in here?'

'I – no, sorry. My shifts run Wednesdays to Saturdays.'

'Anyone else out there work here on Monday?'

'I don't think so. Let me check the roster.'

She moved to an ancient computer that perched on one corner of the desk, typed in a password and then struck the "enter" key with such force that Jan jumped.

'Sorry – it sticks. Probably bits of food stuck between the keys, you know?'

Wrinkling her nose, Jan moved to the woman's shoulder as she scrolled through a list of emails.

Beverley frowned. 'Sorry, nothing here. I can give you a list of names and contact numbers if that helps, but I'll have to get that authorised by the personnel department first. Is that okay?'

'That's perfect,' said Turpin. 'Any chance we could take a look at the camera recordings?'

The duty manager spun her chair around to face him. 'I don't know. I'm supposed to be out there keeping an eye on things. How long do you need?'

'As long as it takes. If we could see the footage from Monday to start with, that'd be a good start. If necessary, we'll have to check the weekend recordings as well.'

The phone on the desk beside Beverley trilled.

'Hang on. Hello?' She sighed. 'I'll be right out.'

Dropping the handset back in the cradle, she

stood and gave an apologetic shrug. 'I have to get back out there. There's a queue stretching back to the door and five cars in the drive-through.'

'Could we make a start while you're sorting them out?' said Jan.

'I don't know.' Beverley's gaze shot to the camera monitors. 'It's probably against the rules. I could get into trouble with head office.'

'How about we take a look to see if there's anything that can help us, and then if we do spot something, we can tell you what we need and you can run that past your bosses?' said Turpin. He shot her a smile. 'It'd be a huge help.'

Jan could see the woman softening under his gaze, and bit her lip.

The phone began to shrill once more, and she saw Beverley's shoulders sag a moment before she spoke.

'All right. But you can't tell anyone.' She pulled out the chair beside the screens and shoved a computer keyboard and mouse towards Turpin. 'This is the recordings menu – you can pull them up by the whole day, or in four-hour time segments. Use these controls to speed it up, slow it down or stop.'

'Thank you,' he said, dropping into the chair.

'Just don't screw up anything,' said the duty manager under her breath, and fled from the room.

'Nice work, Sarge,' said Jan. 'All the charm.'

He chuckled, tapping a series of keystrokes to find the recordings for that Monday, and then looked at his fingers, a look of disgust on his face.

'There's even grease on this.'

'Do you want some gloves?' Jan swung the other chair around next to him and sat, peering at the screen.

'Too late now.'

It took twenty minutes for Turpin to fathom the filing system used by the fast food company for their security footage and then locate the files for Monday morning.

Jan's heart skipped when she saw the time stamp on the first recording. 'Five o'clock in the morning?'

'What time did Tom say the bus ticket was stamped that was found in Matthew's pocket?'

'Hang on.' She reached into her bag, opened her notebook and pulled out her mobile phone at the same time. 'Five forty-five. According to these search results, there's a bus service from Didcot to here that left at five-fifty. That would have dropped him off near Victoria Road just before six-fifteen.'

Turpin went to run a hand over his jaw, then stopped, his mouth twisting as he inspected the grime clinging to his fingertips. 'It's only twenty minutes from Swindon by train.'

He began the playback and soon adjusted the settings until they could watch at double the speed.

The first hour passed by with a skeleton crew of staff members arriving one after the other, and then a steady stream of vehicles appeared at the drive-through. Here and there, various sizes of trucks and vans pulled into the car park, their drivers wandering in wearing high visibility vests and jackets, bundled up against the chill morning air.

Regular customers were easy to spot from the various camera angles that recorded the activities in the restaurant – they paused at the counter to chat with the staff, nodded in greeting to each other and were on their way within minutes, takeout coffees and breakfasts at the ready.

Jan frowned. 'I can't see him yet.'

'We're only up to six o'clock. Too early if he got here on that bus.' Turpin didn't look up from the screen, his hand guiding the mouse across the controls.

She said nothing further, and shuffled in her seat to offset the way her backside was going numb.

After another thirty minutes of footage passed by in a blur, her colleague sat upright and jabbed his finger at the screen.

'It's him.'

They watched Matthew entering the restaurant a little after half past six, holding open the door for two builders while keeping his head down, then walking towards the counter.

Wearing the same clothes as he'd been wearing when he was killed in the alleyway on Monday night, the boy pushed back his hoodie and lifted his chin so he could see the menu displayed above the tills. He appeared to jangle some change in the pocket of his jeans before pulling out his hand and staring at the coins, then stepped forward to the counter.

'He's so young,' said Jan, her voice a murmur. 'Thin for his age, too.'

He placed an order, then when it arrived took his tray across to an isolated spot at the window, away from the rest of the diners. Opening the cardboard burger carton, he tipped his fries inside the lid and stared out at the passing traffic as he nibbled at his food.

Jan brought her hand to her mouth as they watched the boy at the window, wondering what was going through his mind. 'He's nervous, isn't he? My two would've wolfed that lot down in seconds.'

'I think you're right,' said Turpin.

Matthew seemed lost in thought, picking apart his paper napkin as he stared through the glass. After a moment, he took a sip from his drink, then pushed it aside and pulled out a mobile phone, his thumbs moving across the screen in a blur of movement.

'Where's his phone?' said Turpin. 'The search teams haven't found it, and the paramedics didn't find one in his pockets when they were looking for a way to identify him.'

'Dumped? Stolen?'

Matthew shoved his phone in his pocket, glanced out of the window, and froze in his seat.

His brow creased, his mouth dropping open as he slipped from the stool and moved away from the glass, his meal abandoned.

'Where'd he go?' Jan's eyes searched the other monitors and tried to spot the boy from another angle.

'Here.' Turpin jabbed his forefinger at the top right-hand screen.

The boy loitered next to the waste bins, sheltering behind a structural pillar displaying that month's special meal deals while he craned his neck to see beyond the window where he had been sitting moments earlier.

After a moment he crossed the restaurant to the toilets, emerged five minutes later, and then hurried through the front door.

Turpin found the corresponding footage that showed the outside of the restaurant, and they watched in silence as Matthew ran across the car park.

'He didn't come back,' he said, after scrolling

the mouse back and forth over the remaining footage. 'That's all we've got.'

'He saw someone, didn't he?' said Jan. 'Someone he recognised.'

'He must've done. And, given his reaction, it was someone who frightened him.'

CHAPTER FIFTEEN

Easing the cricks from his spine, Mark followed Jan through the staff door and into the restaurant.

The lunchtime service was underway, with a steady stream of vehicles and pedestrians pouring through the premises, and the steady *beep* of the card machines at each of the four tills playing a constant soundtrack alongside shouted orders, loud conversations and the hiss of fryers and grills.

A thick atmosphere of sweat, damp clothing and disinfectant cloyed with the smells emanating from the food preparation area.

The duty manager looked over from where she

was dispensing a soft drink into a large takeaway cup as they drew closer, her eyes registering surprise before she recovered.

'I think she forgot we're here,' said Jan.

'I'm not surprised, given all this.' Mark craned his neck to see over the heads of the people queuing. 'It'll be a while before we can speak to her about getting a copy of that tape. Wait here – there's something I need to do.'

His colleague shot him a quizzical look until he jerked his thumb over his shoulder towards the sign on the door depicting the men's toilet, and then she turned away, her attention taken by a mother trying to balance a wriggling child on her hip while wrestling a litter-laden tray into one of the bins.

Mark smiled as Jan began to help, and then opened the door leading to the toilets.

The noise from the restaurant faded as the automatic closing mechanism hissed shut, and he stood for a moment beside a tiled wall.

Four ceramic sinks lined the room beyond the two hand-dryers beside him, with two urinals and a single cubicle on the opposite side.

Water pooled across the vanity units, splatters

of liquid soap trailing over the surface towards the direction of the dryers, while the tiled floor bore the brunt of mud trodden in over the course of the morning.

Mark wandered into the cubicle and ran his gaze over the wall behind the toilet bowl. The cistern and pipework had been hidden behind a dark slate-coloured panelling, sealing it away and ensuring that the plumbing remained tamper-proof. Unless there was a spanner in the back of the pool car – which he very much doubted – he didn't stand a chance of investigating further.

Walking back towards the washbasins, he turned and surveyed the room, discounting the waste bin in the corner.

'Come on,' he said. 'Where else?'

By his estimation, Matthew was about five foot tall. On the video recording, the fourteen-year-old had spent no more than five minutes in the gents' toilets before reappearing in the restaurant. He had carried no backpack, no luggage, nothing.

Mark exhaled, caught sight of his face in the mirror as he turned, and then froze.

Was it possible?

Rushing towards the cubicle, he glanced over his shoulder towards the exit door and then reached out and flipped down the lid on the toilet seat.

He paused and pulled a pair of protective gloves from his jacket pocket. Moments later, he was balanced with a foot each side of the lid, neck crooked to one side and his palms on the tiles that lined the suspended ceiling.

At six foot two inches, he found the angle awkward, but it would have been well within Matthew's reach.

Mark patted his hand against the tile above the toilet and was rewarded with an eyeful of dust as it came loose from its aluminium frame. Swearing under his breath, wiping at the tears that pricked, he pushed aside the thought of having his fingers nibbled by an errant rodent and lodged his hand into the gap and felt around.

Nothing.

On to the next tile.

He emitted a grunt of surprise when it gave way with little of the drama of the first tile, and thrust his hand into the dark space.

Heart racing, he stumbled on his precarious perch when his fingers touched plastic.

The mobile phone had been hidden on the left-hand side of the tile placement, balanced across the framework in such a way that if any of the tiles were dislodged, it wouldn't fall.

'Yes!'

Mark pulled the phone from its hiding place and climbed to the floor, then jumped.

A large man in his forties – bald, broad, and glaring – stood beside the exit door.

'What are you doing?'

Mark flipped over his warrant card and waved it under the man's nose as he passed. 'Don't forget to flush – and wash your hands.'

He didn't wait for a response.

Jan raised an eyebrow from her position next to the serving counter when he entered the restaurant, a slight colour to her cheeks as he approached. 'Everything all right, Sarge? You were gone a while.'

'Not what you think.' He held up the mobile phone. 'Matthew's.'

'What?'

He placed a hand on her arm and steered her

away from the queue of people at the counter, ignoring the inquisitive stares that followed them.

'Got an evidence bag on you?'

'No, but hang on.' She wandered over to the serving counter, spoke to a girl at one of the tills, and then returned with a paper takeout bag and shook it open. 'This will have to do. Where was it?'

'In the ceiling. It's gone dead, but I think it's the same model as Tom Wilcox uses – hopefully he's got a charger at the station.'

'If he hasn't, someone will. I managed to speak to Beverley – she's going to phone her head office when her shift ends at one o'clock to request they send us a copy of the recordings. I've asked that they include Saturday and Sunday as well, just in case.'

'Thanks. All right – let's get back to the station and find out what's on this phone.'

'Do you want to get something to eat while we're here?'

Mark peered over his shoulder, took one look at the greasy offerings being shoved across the counters towards customers, and shook his head.

'I think I'll pass.'

CHAPTER SIXTEEN

Aiming the key fob over her shoulder, Jan hurried across the police station car park to the security door, swiped her pass card and took the stairs two at a time.

Turpin had gone on ahead, dashing across the road from the fast food restaurant to try to find Ewan Kennedy before he disappeared to Headquarters for the day.

She paused outside the incident room, taking a moment to catch her breath and straighten her jacket, and then stepped into a space that was as loud as it was crowded.

Turpin beckoned to her from the front of the

room where he stood beside Kennedy at the whiteboard, the remaining members of the investigation team dragging chairs across the carpet to form a rough semi-circle.

The DI paced the carpet as the group settled, then called for their attention.

'First of all, I want to say thanks to you all for your dedication over the past two days,' he said. 'We have a lot of information to process, and it might feel as if we haven't made a lot of progress in the time we've had to date, but it's your attention to detail that will see Matthew's killer arrested.'

He let his words settle, and then shook the takeaway bag containing the boy's mobile phone. 'We've now obtained confirmation that when Matthew arrived in Oxfordshire by train on Monday morning, he travelled by bus from Didcot Parkway to Abingdon and then made his way to the fast food restaurant over the road from here. He was seen abandoning his meal before going to the toilet, and then ran from the building a few moments later. Mark found a mobile phone in the suspended ceiling in the gents' toilets, and having seen Matthew on security footage with it before he went to the toilet, we can assume it belongs to him.'

'Tom – have you got your phone charger here?' said Turpin.

'Yes.'

The police sergeant crossed the room and took the phone from Kennedy, then plugged it in at Turpin's desk. He peered at the screen. 'Looks like a cheap pay-as-you-go model. My niece has one like it. Our lad might not have thought to add a passcode if he was planning on dumping it at some point, so we should be able to start processing the data from it as soon as we've got some battery power.'

'Good, thanks,' said Kennedy. 'I want everything you can get.'

'We saw Matthew sending someone a text while he was eating,' said Jan. 'Then he looked out of the window – he looked shocked, as if he recognised someone, and then that's when he shot off to the toilets to hide the phone.'

'Did anyone enter the restaurant and approach him?'

'No – he left the place as soon as he emerged from the toilets,' said Turpin.

'What about after he left?'

'No-one entered the restaurant looking as if they were searching for someone, no.'

'How long until we get the security footage from their head office?'

'I'll chase it up after the briefing, guv. They know it's urgent.'

'Okay. Thoughts about why he dumped the phone,' said the DI. 'Anyone? I mean, my kids are always on theirs – they panic if they're without them for more than thirty seconds. So, why did Matthew leave his behind? More to the point – why hide it where he did?'

Caroline raised her hand. 'Guv, what if he was on the run from whoever he saw through the glass, and thought they'd used his phone to track down his whereabouts? Maybe he thought if he left it behind, he could avoid being followed.'

'Easy enough to do with a tracking app,' said Jan. 'But if he was using a pay-as-you-go phone, would they have had a chance to do that?'

'Yes, if the person who put the tracking app on was the same one who gave him the phone.'

Kennedy wrote the younger detective constable's suggestion on the whiteboard.

'Caroline, work with Tom once that phone's charged up and go through the apps to see what you can find. The location history on the phone as well – it might give us some information about where he's been prior to arriving here, too. Chase up British Transport Police about camera footage on the trains as well,' he said. 'I'll get onto our colleagues at Wiltshire Police and ask them to trace Matthew's movements prior to catching the train. Alex – I want you to speak to the council about CCTV footage for the Marcham Road. We need to find out where Matthew went after he left the fast food restaurant, and whether anyone followed him. Double check that he did arrive on that early bus, too, in order to eliminate someone driving him here.'

'It makes you wonder why he got into Abingdon so early,' said Wilcox. 'After all, if he was trying to sell drugs – based on what we found in his pockets – then he wasn't going to be flush with customers at that time of day, was he?'

'He was young, and there wasn't a lot of money found on him,' said Caroline, holding up her mobile phone. 'I think he was being careful, budgeting for what he needed to do. I've just been looking at the arrival times for trains from Swindon. If he'd arrived any later than he did, it would've cost him twice as much to travel. He came here early because he could afford to.'

'And probably why he chose to eat at the fast food place,' said Kennedy.

'That might not be the case, guv,' said Jan. 'It's more likely that he went there because it was the only place open at that time of the morning. It opens at five o'clock – it gave him somewhere to shelter until he was ready to do whatever he came here to do. Obviously, something happened to make him change his mind, but I think he went to the restaurant on purpose.'

'And then because he ended up abandoning his food, he was hungry again by mid-morning,' said Turpin, 'which is why he then turned up at Angie's café in the square. Hers is one of the cheaper ones in the town centre.'

'But where did he go in the meantime?' said Kennedy. 'And who was he supposed to be selling drugs to when the deal went wrong and he ended up dead?'

Alex raised his hand. 'Guv?'

'Yes?'

The youngest member of the team pulled at the tie at his neck and blushed. 'Well, it's just that Mark and Jan said Matthew was looking out the window while he was eating – before he ran off, I mean.'

'And?' said Kennedy.

'You told us at this morning's briefing that Mark recognised him from the photo taken at the post mortem. What if Matthew was murdered because he was coming here to find Mark? What if he found out he had been transferred here, and wanted to ask for his help?'

Turpin shot the detective constable a look of confusion. 'But how would he know where to find me?'

'You were all over the national news a year ago after the priest murders, Sarge,' said Jan. 'It wouldn't have been difficult.'

'Shit.'

'That window in the fast food restaurant faces the police station, doesn't it?' said Alex, warming to his theory. 'So, what if it was never about doing a drug deal? What if he was just waiting for Mark to turn up to work on Monday morning so he could speak to him?'

CHAPTER SEVENTEEN

Mark hunched over his phone and tapped out a text, his heart heavy.

To his left, two of the team from Force Control on the top floor sat in matching chairs, heads bowed as they spoke in soft tones, their voices blurring with the newsreader's on the large television fixed to the wall.

He ignored the red headline ticker along the foot of the screen, the sound of footsteps as other police personnel passed behind him and the called-out banter that echoed across the mezzanine while the rest of the station carried on as usual.

The station's atrium normally provided a space from which to escape the pressures of work for a few solitary moments. People tended to leave each other alone, appreciating the need to decompress, to be alone.

To worry.

Glancing down at his phone when it vibrated, Mark exhaled as he read the response from Lucy to say everything was all right and that she and his daughters were at the Ashmolean Museum in Oxford.

Nausea clutched at his stomach.

Alex's theory that Matthew's appearance in Abingdon might have been the boy's attempt to seek him out brought other complications with it.

If Matthew was here, who had killed him?

And did that person know that Mark's daughters were here, too?

Now his position within the investigation team was under review, with the DI recalled to Headquarters to meet their superiors and discuss his future.

A shadow fell over his shoulder, and he jerked to one side, heart racing.

'Caroline said I'd find you down here. Are you all right?'

Jan sank onto the sofa next to him, her eyes concerned as she turned to face him. She gestured to his phone. 'Everyone okay?'

'Yes. They're all in Oxford for the day.'

His colleague raised her gaze to the pale grey sky beyond the atrium windows. 'Museums?'

'And shopping, knowing Louise. Especially when she finds the bookshops.'

They fell to silence for a moment, and Mark leaned back against the soft furnishings before running a hand over his face.

'What a fucking mess.'

'It's not your fault, Sarge. Blame the bastard who killed him.'

'If I'd been in on Monday morning instead of having to drive over to Wiltshire to fetch the girls so Debbie could catch her flight, I'd have been here. Matthew would've seen me get to work, wouldn't he?' He twisted around to face her, hearing the urgency in his voice. 'Alex is right – you can see the back of the police station from where he was sitting.'

'That doesn't mean he would've walked

through the front door to speak to you, does it?' Jan sighed, peered over her shoulder as the two Force Control staff left their seats, and then turned her attention back to him. 'Especially as we think he saw someone he knew and ran away. You weren't due in until eight o'clock – he was already gone by then.'

'What if he came back?'

'Then we'll find out when we get the recordings from the restaurant's head office. Until then, you've got to stop blaming yourself for any of this, Mark. Blame the bastards who were using Matthew to traffic drugs. Blame the bastard who stabbed him and left him to die.'

He blinked at the fierceness in her eyes as she spoke, and then shook his head to try to clear the despair that hung over him.

'Have you told Lucy about what happened in Swindon?'

'Yes, she knows.' He grimaced. 'And Louise and Anna haven't mentioned seeing anyone following them lately. I'm probably being paranoid, right?'

'Nothing wrong with that, Sarge. They're your daughters, after all. You've got a right to be worried about them.' Jan cocked her head to one side. 'And having seen what you're like with them, I would imagine they'd tell you straight away if they were worried about anything.'

Pushing his phone into his jacket pocket, Mark stood and straightened his trousers, then forced a smile as he looked at his colleague.

'All right, well I'm still on the team until Kennedy gets back, so let's head back upstairs and see what we can do in the meantime.'

'Sarge?'

Tom's shout carried through the atrium, earning the police sergeant a few startled glares from the personnel who had started to mingle around the television with coffees and snacks. He ignored them and hurried towards Mark and Jan.

'What's wrong?' said Mark.

'We've started to access the information on the mobile phone. Thought you might want to come and see what we've got so far.'

'Lead the way.'

Moments later, Mark hovered at Alex's elbow while the detective constable tilted the phone screen so the small group around his chair could all see.

'He seems to have deleted messages on a regular basis, and the call logs – there are none listed,' he said. 'But whatever happened on Monday morning, he didn't get a chance to do that. Probably in too much of a rush to dump the phone. This is the last text message he sent.'

Mark's jaw clenched as he read the capitalised words on the screen.

LEAVE ME ALONE.

'Who did he send it to?'

'This number, here.' Alex jabbed at the screen with his forefinger. 'There are no saved contacts.'

'Perhaps this is a burner phone, then,' said Jan. 'Not his regular one – if he had one. That would explain why there are no call logs or anything like that. One number in, one number out.'

'Like a direct connection to whoever was using him,' said Mark. 'Alex, can you work on this and see if you can retrieve any deleted messages? At the least, find out how often he was calling or texting to that number, and who it belongs to.'

'Do you want me to phone it?'

'No.'

Mark and Jan spoke in unison, and then he nodded at her to continue.

'Not until we know who it belongs to,' she said to Alex.

'Speaking of which, turn off all the location services and remove any tracking apps on there,' said Tom. 'They found out Matthew was here, so they must've traced him somehow. If that phone was given to him by the person who killed him, or someone who knows the killer, then that was their easiest way of keeping an eye on his movements. We don't want to tip them off that we've got this.'

Mark shook his head as he listened to the sergeant, a new realisation dawning. 'He didn't stand a chance, did he? The minute he left Swindon, he became a target. They were never going to let him go.'

'But, why?' said Jan. 'He was fourteen years old, for Christ's sake. What harm could he do to any of them?'

'I don't know yet,' said Mark. 'But whatever it was, whatever he knew, someone decided he was too much of a risk.'

CHAPTER EIGHTEEN

Mark ducked his head under the beam above a thick wooden door and entered a public bar area that oozed warmth.

The pub on the bridge was quiet at this time of year, with only a few locals using the tables around the fringes of the room and the stools at the bar abandoned.

He turned his attention from the polished and gleaming beer taps at a thunder of shoes across the parquet flooring, and smiled as his youngest daughter reached him.

'Dad!' Anna barrelled into him, her arms wrapping around his waist.

'Oomph.' He fought the urge to take a step back as his old abdominal wound protested, and returned the hug.

'You're late.'

'Sorry. Work stuff.'

She grinned, and he realised with a jolt that she no longer had to lift her chin to meet his gaze.

'Hey, Dad,' Louise called over from a table tucked away in the corner, and gestured to an empty glass. 'Good timing.'

'Bloody cheek.'

'She's got a good point, though.' Lucy held up her wine glass. 'If you're buying...'

Mark reached for his wallet and rolled his eyes as a young woman in her twenties appeared from a door to the left of the bar. 'Whatever they're having and a pint of best, please.'

'No problem,' she said.

Mark handed two soft drinks to Anna and sent her ahead while he paid.

Lucy pushed out the seat next to hers when he reached the table, and he sank into it with a sigh after handing her a glass of wine.

He eyed the remnants of pizza crumbs scattered across the plates before the waitress began to clear them away, and decided he had better pick up an Indian takeaway on his way back to the house.

'Cheers, all,' he said, tapping his glass against theirs. 'Everything all right? What did you get up to in Oxford, then?'

'We saw a dead man,' said Anna.

Mark's glass stopped halfway to his mouth, and he turned to Lucy. 'What?'

She held up her hand and shook her head. 'Don't panic. It was a skeleton in the museum, that's all.'

'Gross.' Anna took a sip of lemonade before peering down her nose. 'I don't know how you do it, Dad.'

'Moving on to happier subject matter, then,' he said, raising an eyebrow as Louise stifled a giggle. 'I take it you managed to fit in some shopping as well?'

He listened, his shoulders starting to relax as his two daughters regaled him about their purchases. He made a mental note to visit an ATM on the way home – he didn't begrudge their buying habits, not when he saw Louise's face while she showed him the books she had discovered in an antiques shop off the High Street, but didn't want to leave Lucy out of pocket, either.

As if reading his thoughts, she reached out for his hand and gave it a quick squeeze.

'Don't worry about it,' she said. 'We'll work it all out when things calm down.'

'Thank you.' He turned his attention to his daughters as they bickered over a game on Louise's mobile phone.

He realised that he had no idea what his daughter used her phone for these days. Debbie had insisted on her having one after the incident in Swindon with the rule that it was only to be used for emergencies. Given that Louise had told him she intended to start applying for part-time jobs as soon as the days grew lighter once more, he wasn't about to argue but his thoughts turned to the way in which Matthew had deliberately hidden his phone.

'Lou?'

His daughter looked up from the screen, her green-grey eyes inquisitive. 'What?'

'How much do you go on social media on that thing?'

'Not much. Mum won't let me, and to be honest none of my friends are allowed so there's no point. I've only got one account to post photos and stuff like that, and that's private anyway.'

'Do you have all the security settings locked down? You know, location and stuff like that.'

'I don't know.' She shrugged. 'I don't think so. Mum was only saying the other day she wanted me to put a tracking app on it.'

'What's that?'

'An app that lets her see where I am. She's going to get one put on her phone, too.' Her face brightened. 'Hey, you could do the same. Then I could see where you are, even when I'm back home.'

'That would be excellent.' Anna folded her arms, her eyes narrowing. 'We could be like spies, Dad.'

They dissolved into giggles, and he forced a laugh. 'All right, well, if you've finished eating and don't want dessert, let's wander back to the boat.'

Yawning, Anna shoved her arms into her thick coat and led the way towards the door.

As he stepped out into the night air, Mark's

breath fogged in front of his face and he let the two girls go on ahead along the narrow pavement, wrapping his hand around Lucy's slender fingers.

'What's on your mind?' she said.

He took a deep breath and watched as Louise paused at the end of the bridge, swung her sister around so their backs were to the stonework and then posed to take a photograph with her phone, the river behind them reflecting the lights from the road and the rear of the pub.

'We think Matthew – the boy who was murdered – might've come to Abingdon on purpose. To find me,' he said. 'And, we think whoever killed him followed him from Swindon.'

Lucy slowed, waiting until the girls had finished larking around and had begun walking towards the footpath that led over the meadow to the narrowboat moorings.

'Do you think his killer is still here?'

'I don't know. It'd be a hell of a risk. The CCTV lot are going through all the footage from Didcot Parkway from Monday morning through to Tuesday to see if they can spot anyone who followed Matthew then leaving after the time of his death, but it's a long shot.'

'You're worried about the girls.'

'I'm worried about all of you.'

'No-one else knows they're here, do they? I mean, it was all very last minute.'

'Debbie would've told the school, and I suppose Gillian – after all, they're meeting up over there to look after their mother. She might've mentioned it to some of her friends, I suppose.'

'No, what I meant was – no-one knows they're with *me*.' She pulled him to a standstill as they reached the towpath, and held her hand against his cheek. 'Everyone thinks they're staying with you, don't they?'

He exhaled, the warmth from her touch heating his jaw as his thoughts slowed and his heart rate gave a lurch. 'I didn't think of that.'

'You've got a lot on your mind at the moment.' She slipped her arm through his as they began to walk towards her narrowboat. 'Leave them with me for now, at least until the end of the weekend. You'll probably have a suspect by then, and you'll have more time to spend with them anyway.'

Mark lifted his gaze to the dark forms of the boats that rocked gently on the current, and saw a block of light shine out from the one at the far end moments before an excited bark reached his ears.

'They have a key to the boat?'

'No, they have my key to the boat. I wanted to take the time to speak to you.' Lucy hugged herself to his side. 'It's getting to you, isn't it? This murder, I mean.'

'I know I couldn't have done anything. It's what I've told myself, it's what I've told other officers in the past but it doesn't help. I can't stop wondering what would've happened if he had managed to speak to me. To ask for my help.'

Lucy took a step closer, then stood on tiptoe and kissed him. 'You'll find who did this, Mark. I know you will.'

He blinked, ran his hand down her arm, and then peered over her curls at the sound of another bark, this time closer.

'At least let me give you some more money before they all eat you out of house and home. The dog included.'

He bent down as Hamish galloped towards them and launched himself at Mark's knees, his paws scrabbling at his trouser legs.

'Hello, boy. Come on then, let's get inside. It's fucking cold out here.'

Lucy laughed. 'Do you want to stay for a drink?'

'Is that okay?'

''Course it is. I've got a Shiraz open. Unless you want something a bit stronger.'

'All right. Just the one, though, and then I'll get out of your way, otherwise those two will never go to bed.'

He stepped over the gunwale and held out his hand to her.

'I wouldn't worry too much,' she said, clambering on board. 'They were out like a light by nine last night – it's all this fresh air they're getting.'

Ducking under the cabin doorframe, he smiled as he caught sight of his daughters curled up next to each other on one of the single berths that lined the main cabin. Louise was still entranced with the game on her phone, but Anna had given up and was reading one of the books her sister had bought that day.

Lucy gestured to the table next to the galley,

then poured two generous measures of wine and handed one to him, her glass clinking against his.

'Have another when you get home,' she said. 'It'll help you sleep.'

'Do you think so?' He took a sip of his drink, savouring the flavours before lowering his voice. 'Maybe. But I'll still worry.'

'I told you. We'll be fine.' Her eyes narrowed as she peered at him over the rim of her glass. 'Besides, Turpin – you're the one I worry about, not them.'

CHAPTER NINETEEN

Despite ignoring Lucy's advice and avoiding a second glass of wine with his takeaway the night before, a bleariness still accompanied Mark as he entered the incident room the next morning.

He sipped from a takeout coffee that he'd bought from a food van parked on Ock Street and tried to batten down his guilt that he had deliberately avoided Angie's café in Market Place, despite it being on his route from home to the police station.

He didn't want to face the questions that would no doubt have been peppered at him while he waited, because he didn't have any answers to give.

Almost three days now, and the locals were getting impatient. People wanted justice for the young boy, newspapers demanded updates, and he knew there would be phone calls from Headquarters wanting the same, before pointed questions were aimed at them by local politicians and councillors.

Caroline looked over her computer monitor as he passed her desk, and he pointed to Jan's empty chair.

'Where's West?'

'Her and Alex have gone into Oxford for the post mortem. It isn't until early afternoon but Kennedy has them interviewing a couple of people who were at the fair on Monday night first – uniform haven't managed to get to them yet. '

He slung his coat over a makeshift rack behind the detective constable. 'Who's doing the post mortem?'

'Michael Ferguson. He's usually based further north, but apparently Gillian's not around…'

Mark nodded and turned away, not wishing to go into details about the pathologist's absence.

Some of his colleagues knew that the forensic specialist was his ex-wife's sister, but it was none of his business to talk about their mother's sudden illness and their quick departure to Jersey.

'Okay, what else is going on?'

Caroline held up a stack of notes that she'd squashed into a haphazard bundle. 'Latest calls from potential witnesses. People who have decided they've remembered seeing something on Monday night since seeing the news, that sort of thing.'

'Or social media.'

'And that.'

'Anything of use?'

She dropped the bundle and scowled. 'No. Most of it regurgitates what they've seen or heard. When I spoke to half of them, they wanted to know what I could tell them, like we're a bloody news service.'

'Anything back from Wiltshire about Matthew's home situation?'

'We got an update through just after you left last night.' Caroline reached out for a stapled report in her tray and handed it over. 'His full name is Matthew Arkdale. He's been in care homes on and off for the past three years – his dad walked out when he was eighteen months old, and his mum's had some problems that meant she couldn't look after Matthew properly. Then, about fourteen months ago she was diagnosed with terminal cancer. She died in a hospice back in March.'

Mark swallowed as he ran his gaze over the text. 'Poor bugger. Any sign of his dad?'

Caroline took the report from him and slung it back in the tray. 'Nothing yet, and I'm not holding my breath—'

A steady bleat from a phone ringing interrupted her, and Mark shot across to his desk, snatching up the receiver before it went to voicemail.

'DS Turpin.'

'Mark? It's Denise in Control.'

'What's up?'

'Thought you might want to know – one of our uniformed patrols just attended a call-out to a clothing shop that backs onto Queen Street. They've had an engineer in to fix their reverse-cycle air conditioning unit this morning – the bloke's found a knife in the motor unit on the back of the building.'

Mark's heart rate ratcheted up a notch. 'Are they still on scene?'

'Yes, and I'm about to send another patrol car over there to help secure it while it's all processed. Do you want a lift with them?'

'I'll meet them in the car park – thanks.' Mark dropped the phone into its cradle and called to Caroline. 'We might have the murder weapon – come on.'

CHAPTER TWENTY

Mark hovered at the fringes of the makeshift cordon that taped off the loading doors of the clothing shop and craned his neck to watch while three CSI investigators worked, a fourth speaking to a pair of uniformed police constables who ensured no-one breached the work area.

'Sarge?'

He turned at Caroline's voice to see her approaching with a man dressed in a blue sweatshirt and jeans, his baseball cap bearing the logo of a local air conditioning company.

'This is John Boxley – he's the chap who discovered the knife.'

'Figured the best thing to do was call your lot.' The tradesman lifted his baseball cap and flattened down his thinning hair.

In his late fifties, he had the posture of someone who spent time crawling into restricted spaces, stooping as if he was about to hit his head.

'Good thinking, Mr Boxley,' said Mark. 'When was the last time the unit was serviced?'

Boxley grimaced. 'God knows – not by us, that's for sure. We put a sticker on the side of the units we work on to remind customers when to call us, and we have a central database with all that information on it too in case they forget.' He jerked his thumb over his shoulder. 'The manager of the shop – Tara – was telling me she's been asking their landlord to replace the unit for over a year because it keeps breaking down.'

'But this is the first time you've been called out to fix it?'

The tradesman squashed his cap back on his head and gave Mark a sardonic smile. 'I think the landlord fell out with the last lot who came out.'

'Okay. Tell me what happened this morning, from when you arrived.'

'I parked my van over there, walked around

and found Tara, then started working on the system inside. It's all linked through the ceiling and then ventilates out the back over there. And that's the main motor for the whole system as well.'

'Is it on all the time?'

'No – she told me they turn it off when they leave to save money.'

'How would someone hide a knife inside?'

'Easy,' said Boxley. 'The vents are quite wide, so you could stick something through if you wanted. The modern units are safer, so the vents are narrower, but that old thing? You could hide your bloody grandmother if you wanted to.'

'Back to this morning…'

'Yeah, so I realised the problem was with the motor, so I switched off the system and came out here. Took me about ten minutes to get the screws loose off the panel but I could hear something vibrating against the casing while I was testing it. As soon as I got the panel off, I could see why – and that's when I stopped and called 999. I figured it might have something to do with that kid's murder on Monday night.'

'Did you touch the knife?'

Boxley frowned. 'I didn't pick it up – I might have knocked it by accident while I was removing the panel though.'

'Not to worry. You did the right thing, thank you. If you could leave your contact details with my colleague here, we'll be in touch with regards to a formal statement.'

Mark left the tradesman with Caroline, and then walked around the cordon to where two of the CSIs were packing away equipment.

He called over to the investigator who had been dusting the outer casing of the unit for fingerprints. 'Anything of use?'

The man waited until he had drawn level with Mark, wrapping the crime scene tape around his hands as he walked before handing it to one of the constables. 'We'll take samples from the chap who was fixing the thing, as well as the staff to eliminate them, but don't hold your breath. You can imagine the dirt and dust that's accumulated.'

'What about the knife?'

'There's blood on the blade consistent with it being used to stab someone – we'll pass it on to the lab to confirm if it's a match with the victim's, but don't get your hopes up about fingerprints.'

'Gloves?'

'Or a coat sleeve pulled down over the attacker's hand.'

'Okay, thanks. We'll let you finish here.'

'Cheers, Sarge. I'm sure Jasper will be in touch soon.'

Mark shoved his hands in his pockets and wandered back to where Caroline waited beside the patrol car that had delivered them to the scene. 'Did you speak to the shop manager?'

'Yes, and uniform have already taken her statement,' she said. 'There are no CCTV cameras out this way, though. They only have cameras inside the shop.'

'Shit.' Mark squinted up at the buildings that surrounded the dead-end street. 'Well, the footage we've managed to get from around here is still being processed back at the station so we'll have to hope one of the cameras around here picked up whoever dumped that knife.'

'You think it's the one that was used to kill Matthew?'

'It's too much of a coincidence otherwise, isn't it?'

CHAPTER TWENTY-ONE

Shaun Mansell twitched the net curtain away from the window above the kitchen sink, and peered out at the driveway of the adjacent property as a car engine revved.

He scratched at the stubble covering his chin and ducked his head to the side to see through the dirt-covered glass.

Cobwebs clung to the corners of the cheap plastic frames the builders had installed when the flats were constructed thirty years ago, and a cold draught poked under the seal. Thick dust covered the windowsill while a dead moth lay upended halfway along with its legs poking up in the air.

Shaun reached to the back pocket of his faded jeans, then cursed under his breath as he remembered emptying the blister pack of pills the night before.

He tugged down the sleeves of his sweatshirt and swayed on his feet, an aching tiredness seizing his eyes.

Would it always be like this now, the constant fear?

Unable to sleep, he had spent the past three days watching the street from his bedroom or the neighbouring property through this window, pacing back and forth, back and forth. Every person who walked past was a threat, every vehicle causing panic.

As he turned his attention to the woman who emerged from the passenger seat of the car below, her long legs accentuated by the skinny jeans and knee-high boots she wore, Shaun's top lip curled at the sight of her boyfriend behind the wheel.

She deserved better than him – he had heard their arguments through the open window of their living room over the summer, their flat directly opposite his on the third floor, and wondered why she stayed with him.

Satisfied the couple posed no threat – for now – he dropped the curtain back into place with a shaking hand. The light caught his wristwatch and he swore as a spasm wracked his spine.

The painkillers were strong, and the doctor had warned him repeatedly about the dangers of overdosing.

That was why he self-medicated.

That was how they found him.

Looking out of the window, either in here or in his bedroom overlooking the street, was a habit born of a paranoia that clawed at his thoughts and occupied every waking moment.

He hadn't eaten for days.

Not since—

'Are you going to go out and get us some food, or what?'

The voice jerked him from his thoughts and he spun around to see a thickset man in his late twenties glaring at him as he leaned against the door frame, an open bottle of whisky in his hand.

Dean Evans had turned up on Monday morning with a backpack, a handful of twenties – and instructions.

Shaun had never seen the man before, but Evans knew everything about him.

Everything.

And then Evans had told him what he was expected to do if he wanted his drug-taking habit kept a secret from his family.

Shaun bit back bile at the memory. 'I'm not hungry. I told you that this morning. It's not my fault if you've eaten everything in the fridge.'

'Just order me something off one of those food apps.'

'I haven't got a card I can use. It's maxed out this month until I get my benefits. I can't get anything at the moment.' Shaun pulled his mobile phone from the back pocket of his jeans and looked at the screen. 'I could show you a map, though. Show you where the supermarket is.'

Dean Evans sneered at him. 'You tosser. D'you think I've got time to go shopping? I'm a busy man, Mansell.'

'Well, I can't. What if someone sees me? What if they find out it was me—'

'They won't.'

'How do you know?'

'Because I do.'

A new fear sent a shiver down his spine. 'Have you done this before?'

'None of your business, sunshine.' Dean handed him some cash, then jerked his thumb over his shoulder. 'I'm going to watch the telly and have a drink. Get me some food, Mansell.'

The man turned his back, a snake tattoo curling from the neck of his T-shirt towards his hairline.

'Dean—'

'What?'

'I'm out of painkillers,' said Shaun, hating the desperation in his voice. 'I'm going to need something to keep me going.'

Pausing in the hallway, Dean frowned for a moment. 'Have you still got the pills you took off the kid?'

Shaun pointed to the small plastic bag next to a grease-covered toaster on the worktop. 'Some dropped out, but there are a few left.'

'Take them, then.'

'Are they safe?'

Dean grinned. ''Course they are. I'll fix you a drink to wash 'em down with.'

CHAPTER TWENTY-TWO

Jan shivered in the pale blue light that filled the examination room, and stared at the floor as a whirring sound reverberated in her skull.

Clenching her teeth, she held her breath as a surge of helplessness and anger filled her chest.

She had managed to keep quiet upon meeting the pathologist who was attending in place of Gillian Appleworth, but his reputation had preceded him.

Despite his experience, Michael Ferguson was not one of the usual pathologists who would carry out an examination on a child – and it showed.

In his early sixties, the pathologist was what

her mother would have referred to as "old school", and possessed none of the empathy that Gillian brought to her work.

Instead, he had spent the first twenty minutes lecturing Alex with a sneer in his voice on the vagaries of performing a post mortem on a young boy, moving the child's limbs with a briskness that grated with Jan as she watched.

When Ferguson reached for the rib shears, both detectives had turned away as the pathologist had continued his work, dictating into a lapel microphone in a tone that conveyed boredom rather than a will to lend some decorum to the proceedings.

'Bloody hell,' Alex murmured under his breath. 'Gillian might be terrifying sometimes, but at least you know she cares.'

Jan said nothing, but bowed her head in agreement.

On the table beyond where she and Alex stood, Michael Ferguson switched off the saw and laid it on a trolley with a clatter before clearing his throat.

'Neither of you are going to learn anything standing over there,' he said, his tone brusque. 'I don't know how Gillian runs her post mortems, but I expect investigating officers to show an interest in what's going on.'

Jan glared at him. 'Gillian tends to treat her guests with a bit more respect. Especially the dead ones.'

The pathologist's mask fluttered as he huffed an exasperated sigh in response. 'Shall we continue?'

She watched as he moved around Matthew's body, probing and removing the vital organs before passing them to Gillian's assistant, Clive Moore, to be tested and weighed.

Finally, after what seemed an eternity, Ferguson lifted his chin and stood back from the examination table.

'Right, well, I can confirm cause of death was this second stab wound to the abdomen. The first one—'

'Wait. What?' Jan moved closer, brushing past Clive as he began to wash the boy's body. 'There are *two* stab wounds?'

'Yes,' said Ferguson. He joined her, and rolled the boy onto his side. 'You can see the first one here. That almost penetrated his kidney, which would have been enough to kill him in my opinion, given how long it took before anyone found him. However, it seems his attacker thought otherwise – the second one pierced his liver.'

Jan shuddered. 'Any signs of a struggle?'

'There's bruising to his shoulder, here.'

'So he could've been grabbed from behind?'

'That could be the case, yes.' Ferguson set the boy on his back once more. 'Or, his attacker stabbed him, then placed a hand on his shoulder to force him to turn around. Then, he was stabbed here, in the abdomen, with the knife thrust at an upwards angle. He didn't stand a chance, I'm afraid. Have you found the weapon?'

'Only this morning,' said Jan. 'And it's an ugly one.'

'Yes, well, I could've told you that from the wounds. Serrated edge, similar to a hunting knife or similar. And all too common these days.' He wiped his gloves down the front of his protective gown. 'We'll run some tests on his organs – all the usual ones, plus toxicology to see if he was partaking of his own supplies.'

'We don't know yet that he was dealing

drugs,' said Jan, unable to keep the tension from her voice. 'He's a victim, no matter what.'

'Yes, well, they're not always as innocent as they look, are they, detective?' The pathologist gestured to Clive. 'All right, stitch him up. We're done here.'

He turned and snapped off his gloves, tossing them into a biohazard bin behind a row of sinks. Twisting the faucet, he began to scrub at his hands, and then peered over his shoulder. 'Off you go. I'll make sure your DI has my report in due course.'

Dismissed, Jan led the way out of the examination room and turned to Alex as the door swished shut.

'What an arsehole,' he said.

'I know, but look – I suppose he's good at his job. Everyone has a different way of dealing with it.'

Alex snorted, then shook his head. 'If you say so. Meet you by the car?'

'Sounds good.'

She waited until her colleague had disappeared through the door to the men's changing room, and then shoved her way into the ladies' and stripped off the protective overalls.

Bundling them into a bin and straightening her suit trousers, she sank onto a wooden bench beneath a line of coat hooks and rested her elbows on her knees.

Despite the conciliatory words she had shared with Alex, she fumed inside. With a shaking hand, she pulled her mobile phone from her bag and hit the speed dial.

'Hi, love. Hang on a minute.'

Scott's voice was drowned out by the drone of power tools, and she winced at the reminder of what had taken place in the examination room. She pinched her nose, trying to block out the remnant stench of death, and closed her eyes.

'Okay, I'm outside.' Her husband sounded out of breath. 'Three flights of stairs and no lift. Got to love these old blocks of flats. How did it go?'

'Awful.' Jan opened her eyes and straightened, tilting her head back until her skull met the plaster wall of the changing room. She stared at the ceiling, her thoughts tumbling. 'Bloody awful.'

'Ferguson on form?'

'In his element. Honestly, thank goodness he

only deals with the dead.' She sighed. 'We're heading back to the station now, but I'll pick the boys up from school today.'

'If you're sure?'

'Yes. Turpin's got my number if he needs me in a hurry.'

'All right. There's a bottle of Pinot Noir in the rack – why don't we crack that open later on?'

She smiled. 'That would be good.'

'Are you going to be okay?' Concern flooded his voice.

'I will be. You know how it is. The young ones always get to me.'

'I know. I love you.'

'Love you too.'

Jan ended the call, wiped at the corners of her eyes, and shoved the phone back into her bag. Standing, she brushed off the back of her trousers, checked her make-up in the mirror over the sink, and then crossed to the door.

Alex was standing in the corridor checking text messages. He glanced up when he saw her approaching and fell into step beside her.

'I don't want to do too many of those,' he said.

'Post mortems are hideous as it is, without it being for a kid.'

'I know,' said Jan. 'Do you have someone at home, Alex? In case you need to talk about it?'

The younger detective shook his head. 'No. My girlfriend's a bit too squeamish to be honest. She doesn't like to hear about stuff like that.'

She rested her hand on his arm as they approached the car.

'Then call me if you need to. You're right – it was hideous.'

CHAPTER TWENTY-THREE

Mark turned up the collar of his coat and eyed the gargoyles that lined the stone buildings of the Guildhall as he walked beneath the ornate archway.

Bloated faces with bulging eyes and squashed noses created grotesque caricatures; effigies of men, animals and mythical creatures that glared at him from their perches and seemed to pass judgment upon him. Two wore wigs, similar to those he had seen in court over the years, and as he turned left into Abbey Close and made his way towards home, his thoughts returned to the murder enquiry and the justice he sought for the young boy left to die alone in a rain-soaked alleyway.

He had spent the afternoon on the phone, jostling for attention at the specialist laboratory that was now processing the knife found in the air conditioning unit, and arguing his case against two other urgent investigations that demanded the technicians' attention. With some reluctance, the case manager had agreed, but only once Mark had sworn never to tell anyone.

With no sign of Jan, he had spent the remainder of his shift in DI Kennedy's office, detailing the steps taken in the investigation to date in order to justify the additional staffing levels that were crucial to maintain during the early stages of their enquiries. Any loss in momentum now would be a disaster, and Kennedy had ensured their report summary set out their concerns before emailing it to Headquarters.

Exhausted, Mark had left the incident room to spend some time with his daughters, helping Anna with the homework that had been set for the half-term holidays while Lucy and Louise laughed and joked in the small galley of the narrowboat and concocted a chilli con carne that had almost blown the roof off his mouth.

As he turned into the Radley Road, his phone began to vibrate in his pocket. He extracted it with a mixture of reluctance and foreboding, wanting nothing more than to get indoors and sink into one of the armchairs with a cold beer before falling asleep.

He didn't recognise the number.

'DS Mark Turpin.'

'Mark? It's Scott. Jan's other half.'

'Scott. Everything all right?'

'Not really. Do you think you could pop over?'

'Now?'

'Please.'

———

'I don't know what to say to her, Mark.' Scott closed the front door and lowered his voice. 'I wanted to wait until the boys were in bed before I phoned you. No sense in them getting upset.'

'Where is she?'

'Out the back.'

'In the garden?' Mark paused, his hand hovering over the buttons of his jacket. 'In this weather?'

'She said she needed some time to think.' Scott ran a hand over his bald pate. 'I'm sorry – I didn't know who else to call. I've only seen her like this once before, and that was after a bad traffic accident that involved kids. She takes it hard with the young ones.'

Mark exhaled. 'The post mortem this morning?'

'Yes. She picked up the boys earlier from school and seemed okay when I got home from work. It's only since they went up to bed that she's – I don't know – I don't know what to say to her to make it better.'

The anguish in the other man's voice and his pained expression cut through any awkwardness Mark felt at being summoned to his colleague's home.

He pointed towards the kitchen. 'Is it okay to go through?'

'Of course. Do you want a glass of wine to take out with you?'

'Go on, then. Thanks.'

Moments later, glass in hand, Mark left Scott emptying the dishwasher and opened the back door. Cold air pinched his earlobes, and he shivered at the drop in temperature compared with the warm kitchen.

Scott and Jan's house was a semi-detached building that had been lovingly restored by the couple over the years. A patio had been laid outside the back door that led to a square lawn, a lone football abandoned in the middle by the twin boys.

His colleague sat bundled up in a thick wool coat at a wrought-iron patio table, her figure silhouetted against a trellis adorned with hanging lanterns that rocked in the breeze.

As he drew closer, he caught the unmistakable whiff of nicotine and spotted a tendril of smoke escape as she exhaled.

'Evening, Sarge.'

She used the toe of her ankle boot to push out the chair next to hers, and waited while he sat.

He took a sip of the wine, smacked his lips and put the glass next to hers. 'You two always pick the good stuff.'

'Did Scott call you?'

'He's worried about you.'

'I know.' She sniffed, then took another drag of the cigarette. 'It's hard to explain, isn't it, when they don't do the job? Sometimes it's easier to be quiet.'

'Only sometimes, Jan.' An itch began at the back of his throat, and he coughed. 'I didn't know you smoked.'

'I don't. Well, I do, but only in emergencies. Like now. The boys don't know, though.'

Mark turned in his seat and peered at the upstairs windows.

'Their bedrooms are at the front, don't worry.'

He twisted back around to face her. 'How was it?'

'Not the same without Gillian.' Jan stubbed out the cigarette, jabbing it into the base of her ankle boot. She wrinkled her nose. 'I know Ferguson is good at what he does, but he lacks heart. We have a dead fourteen-year-old who was malnourished and homeless, and—'

'He was too businesslike?'

'Exactly.' She picked up her wineglass and took a sip. 'Did you know it was the Runaway Fair on Monday night?'

'Runaway?'

'It dates back a few hundred years. Labourers used to go along to the Michaelmas Fair the previous week to try to find a new landowner to work for. If it turned out to be a lousy deal, they could come back the next week to the Runaway Fair to find someone else instead.' She pulled the collar of her coat around her neck, her voice wistful. 'I can't help thinking that's what Matthew was trying to do. Run away. Find someone else to look after him. A new start. And instead, whoever he was running away from found him, and killed him…'

She broke off, and shook her head before looking away, blinking.

Her phone buzzed, and Mark saw a notification pop up on the screen.

'Alex.' Jan ran her finger over the phone, opened the message, and gave a sad smile. 'I told him to call me if he needed to talk about today – I think it was the first time he's had to attend for a child's death.'

'Is he okay?'

'Seems so. He says he's having a beer and watching a trashy action film.'

'It's good of you to keep an eye on him.'

She shrugged, and pushed the phone away. 'It's what I do, isn't it? Mother everyone.'

'Thank goodness.' He smiled. 'We'd fall apart without you. We'd certainly starve, anyway.'

That elicited a laugh, and he let his shoulders relax.

She drained her glass, then stood and reached out her hand. As he took it in hers and squeezed, she nodded.

'Thanks, Sarge. I'll be okay, don't worry.'

CHAPTER TWENTY-FOUR

Jan entered the incident room the next morning with a renewed determination that was buoyed by the energy emanating from the rest of the team as she strode towards her desk.

She greeted Turpin, switched on her computer and spent the next fifteen minutes sifting through the phone messages that had been left overnight. She looked up as Ewan Kennedy walked out of his office, loosening his tie.

'Briefing, everyone. Lots to get through, so let's not hang about.'

'We finally got the list of council-owned properties through late yesterday,' said Turpin under his breath as they made their way to the end of the room and found chairs close to the whiteboard.

'Bloody took them long enough,' she said, then turned to Kennedy as he opened the meeting.

The detective inspector glanced at his notes, then peered over his reading glasses at the assembled team.

'The focus for today is to hone in on those people already identified by Tom and his team as being vulnerable within the local community and finding out if any of them saw our victim in the weeks leading up to his murder,' he said. 'My thanks to uniform for the diligence in providing this information, and for the ongoing support to this enquiry. A copy of this list has been emailed to each of you – is that correct, Tracy?'

'Yes, guv,' said the administrative assistant. 'Names, addresses, and a summary of actions taken to date, including any previous charges and custodial sentences.'

'Guv?' Tom raised his hand. 'My officers have known some of these people for a long time. Most are addicts, and have been for a number of years. Often, they're in no state to protect themselves from these gangs, which leaves them open to exploitation.'

'Tread softly, you mean?' said Kennedy, with no trace of malice in his voice. 'Okay, noted – thanks. Right, you lot – you heard him. If these people are being used by gangs to hide a county lines operation, then they're going to be scared as well as disorientated from whatever substances they're taking. However, we owe it to Matthew to find out who knew about his being in Abingdon, and whether he was meant to make his way to one of these properties as a cuckoo in order to deal drugs from here. Caroline – have you got the list of privately owned properties?'

'Here, guv.' Caroline waved a sheaf of paper. 'There's a copy in HOLMES2 for everyone to access. I also asked local letting agencies whether there had been any issues in the past with these properties, and five tenants have been flagged as potential cuckooing victims. I think Tom's familiar with a couple of these?'

The police sergeant peered over her shoulder, and nodded. 'Yes, no surprises there.'

'All right, add them to the list,' said Kennedy. He began to pace the carpet tiles in front of the whiteboard. 'We're going to do this a little differently today, ladies and gentlemen. Given that uniform are familiar with these people, we're going to let Tom and his team run the house-to-house searches today. That way, we'll get through the list faster. I also want the neighbours interviewed, just in case the tenants on this list are too scared to talk. The rest of you I want on hand here so if uniform find information or persons relevant to this investigation, you can deal with it immediately. Tracy will hand out the rosters after this briefing. Any questions?'

Jan kept her head bowed, her pen dashing across her notebook as she jotted down the finer points of the morning's planned operation, listening to her colleagues as the details were expanded upon and finessed.

She lifted her head as Kennedy called for quiet, and paused beside the whiteboard.

'Next item,' he said, and held up a stapled report. 'The specialist laboratory has provided its preliminary findings in relation to the toxicology of the pills found in Matthew's pocket. I'll save you reading through the chemical analysis – they're telling us this is a new form of benzodiazepine, and more potent than the typical street blues our colleagues across the country are having to deal with.'

A shocked silence followed his words, and then Alex spoke.

'Have they seen it before?'

'No,' said Kennedy. 'This is a new one, and according to the summary in this report, it's lethal at a much smaller dose than street blues. Add in alcohol, methadone or any opiate, and it will kill rather than cause a non-fatal overdose.'

He tossed the report onto the desk next to him, and crossed his arms over his chest. 'So, why was Matthew carrying it?'

'And, where's the rest?' said Turpin. 'Only three were found in his pocket. If he was sent here as part of a county lines operation to start dealing, then someone has the missing pills.'

'Exactly.' The DI ran a hand over his chin. 'Tom – add the photographs of the pills that were found to the packs you're handing out to your team so they can ask around while they're doing the house-to-house enquiries this morning. Find out if anyone has seen these pills before, or whether anyone has heard about a new type of benzodiazepine on the market.'

'We could make some calls to the local homelessness and addiction services as well,' said Jan. 'If these pills are already in circulation, they could be seeing the after-effects.'

'Do that, and send a summary of the toxicology report to all local hospitals and doctors' surgeries as well,' said Kennedy. 'Okay, everyone – dismissed. We'll have a further briefing this afternoon at six o'clock. Let's hope we have some bloody answers by then.'

CHAPTER TWENTY-FIVE

Mark slapped the side of the photocopier with the palm of his hand and swore as the machine juddered to a standstill, the distinct smell of burnt toner filling the incident room.

He backed away, wafting the air with the papers he had managed to retrieve from the guts of the printing machine and then looked around with faint embarrassment.

Tracy grinned from where she sat at her desk, then took pity on him and made her way over to where he lingered.

'Broken it, Sarge?'

'I bloody hope not.' He held up the remnants

of the document, the corners chewed and mangled. 'Kennedy wants all this on his desk before he heads over to Headquarters at twelve.'

She rested her hands on her hips, ran a critical eye over the photocopier, and then held out her hand for the scraps of paper. 'Give it here. I think I know what the problem is.'

'You're an admin ninja, Trace. I knew it.'

'And my price is a cup of tea, Sarge. Milk, strong, no sugar.'

'Coming right up.'

He left her pulling various drawers and panels apart, gathered up his and Jan's empty cups and headed off to the kitchenette, battening down his frustration.

They had spent the morning listening to the reports coming in from the uniformed patrols conducting the house-to-house enquiries, but frustration at the lack of a breakthrough was starting to fray his nerves.

Caroline and Alex had taken one of the radios and headed down to the atrium for a break, taking advantage of the lull in activities in the incident room, along with a stack of statements and reports they were still trying to digest.

So far, none of the feedback from uniform was helping.

No-one had seen Matthew in the days leading up to his death, nor in the hours before.

No-one recognised him from the photograph that had been shown to each person on the list Tom Wilcox and his team had drawn up.

The telephones remained silent, and with half the investigation team out pursuing other enquiries, an uneasiness filled the incident room while they waited for new information.

Mark wandered back with the steaming mugs of tea, passed one to Tracy and hurried back to his desk as his mobile phone began to ring.

'DS Turpin.'

'Mark, it's Jasper here.' The CSI lead's voice sounded breathless, excited. 'We've just had an email from the specialist laboratory about the knife that was found.'

'Christ, that was quick.' Mark shoved Jan's tea towards her, then leaned forward and slid his notebook closer, popping the top off a pen with his teeth. 'What've you got?'

'A name in the system, based on an eighty per cent likelihood of a match with the fingerprints.

Shaun Mansell. I ran a quick search online and found some news articles from three years ago. Looks as if he drove into someone's garden wall while high on cocaine. No-one else was injured, but he was lucky to escape with his life. He was in hospital for a few weeks before he could make it to court.'

Mark frowned. 'It's a long way from a drug-related car crash to stabbing a kid to death.'

'That's why I thought I'd phone you rather than make you wait until you got the finished report later today.'

'Okay, hang on.' Mark hit the "mute" button and held up his notebook to Jan. 'Can you run a check on this Shaun Mansell? Jasper says there's an eighty per cent chance his fingerprints match the partials found on the knife.'

She bent her head to her computer screen as he returned to his call.

'Jan's running his name through the system to see what we've got,' he said. 'Was it definitely the knife used to murder Matthew?'

'That's what the blood samples lead us to believe, yes,' said Jasper. 'I don't know whose arse Kennedy kicked to get this lot over to me before the weekend, but that's got to be a record turnaround these days.'

Mark grinned. 'I'd imagine he'll suffer the consequences next time – there's always someone in the area demanding fast results, not just him.'

'Funny, that's what the bloke at the lab said.'

'Mark?' Jan raised her hand to catch his attention. 'I've found him. Shaun Mansell, twenty-eight. He's in the system for burglary offences, plus a driving offence from three years ago. Apparently, he suffered severe injuries but no-one else was hurt, and the judge took pity on him so he didn't have to serve a custodial sentence. He registered with a local social services programme for recovering addicts a month after the court hearing.'

'Anyone keeping an eye on him?' said Mark.

'Last update on here is from PC Brandon Hall. It's dated early September.'

'All right, thanks. Jasper? We'll let you get on – thanks for the phone call.'

'No problem. I'll forward on the lab report with my summary by the close of business today and I'll copy it to Kennedy to keep him in the loop.'

'Thanks.'

Mark shoved his mobile in his jacket pocket. 'Okay, where do we find Brandon Hall?'

'On holiday.' Tracy wandered across to where they sat, handed Mark a sheaf of stapled documents that were warm to the touch, and sank into a spare chair beside his desk. 'Not back until Wednesday next week.'

'Who's he usually rostered with?' said Jan.

The administrative assistant's brow puckered for a moment, and then her eyes lit up. 'I remember – Alice Fields. I've seen her around today. Hang on – back in a moment.'

Five minutes later, a petite police constable in her early twenties followed Tracy across the incident room towards them, and turned her attention to Mark after the introductions were made.

'Tracy said you wanted to know about one of the users Brandon keeps an eye on?'

'Yes – Shaun Mansell.'

Alice choked out an exasperated huff. 'Oh, him. Pain in the arse, to be honest. You know the sort – he says he's a reformed addict, and preaches to anyone who'll listen how he's learned the error of his ways.'

'Has he?'

Alice gave a bitter laugh. 'No – he's just switched cocaine for prescription painkillers, and the place stank of weed – although he denied it. What do you need him for, anyway, Sarge? If you don't mind me asking, that is.'

'We think he's linked to the murder of Matthew Arkdale on Monday night.'

The police constable's eyes widened in reply.

'What do you know about him? Does he work anywhere?' said Jan.

'Not as far as I'm aware, no. He manages to get by on whatever handouts he gets from the government because of his injuries from the car crash, and that's about it, although I'm sure he's earning a bit of cash on the side here and there.'

'Dealing drugs?'

'Not that we're aware of.'

'You mentioned he's on painkillers – do you know what for?' said Mark.

'A bad back. Something to do with the injuries he sustained in the car crash,' said Alice. 'I've seen him on days when he says the pain is bad and

THE LOST BOY   199

I don't think he was acting. You could see it in his eyes.'

'Do you know where he lives?'

'A flat on the other side of town – although he said social services keep threatening to kick him out. Apparently his neighbours complain about the loud music.'

'What's Brandon's connection with him?'

'Brandon was on duty the night Shaun drove through that brick wall and crawled into the car to stay with him until the ambulance arrived. Says he was lucky to be alive, and that he reckons his addiction wasn't helped by the amount of painkillers he had to take after the accident. We check in on him every few weeks to make sure he's keeping out of trouble if we're passing.' Alice turned down the volume on her radio as it spat out a hiss of static. 'You know what some of us are like – pet projects, and all that.'

'When did you last see him?' said Turpin.

'A couple of days before Brandon went on his round-the-world trip,' said Alice. 'So, about the beginning of September.'

'And nothing since?'

'No. I've been too busy.' She shrugged. 'You

know what it's like. It's just Brandon who wants to keep an eye on some people before they get into trouble again.'

Mark pulled back his shirt cuff and checked his watch. 'When does your shift end?'

'In about two hours.'

'Do me a favour? Find someone to go with you and bring in Shaun for questioning.'

'Okay, Sarge.'

'Thanks.'

As the constable left the room, her radio to her lips while she informed Control of her changed plans, Jan drained her mug of tea and set it down on the desk.

'Do you think he might know something?'

'I don't know,' said Mark. 'But if he does, and he wasn't on Tom's list because he's been behaving himself recently, who else have we missed?'

CHAPTER TWENTY-SIX

Jan was halfway through writing up a report summary to accompany Turpin's paperwork for DI Kennedy when her phone rang, ruining her train of thought.

'Bugger.' She sighed, glared at her screen in the vain hope that the words would magically appear on their own, then reached out to answer the call. 'West.'

'It's Tom Wilcox, downstairs,' said the familiar voice. 'Got a chap here by the name of Douglas Jones. Said he was asked to come here and speak to you by his boss.'

She frowned, reached out for her notebook and frantically flicked through the pages, trying to remind herself of the name.

As if anticipating her confusion, Wilcox cut into her thoughts. 'He was working with Sheila Cook at Didcot Parkway on Monday morning.'

'Perfect,' said Jan, closing her notebook and waving her hand at Turpin who was on another call. 'Could you let him know we'll be right down?'

'No problem – I'll book you into interview room four. We haven't had anyone in there today, so it's the cleanest one of all of them.'

'Owe you one, thanks.'

Turpin finished his call at the same time she put her phone back into its cradle.

'Douglas Jones is downstairs,' she explained, pulling her jacket off the back of her chair. 'He's the one Sheila Cook said was working platform two at Didcot on Monday morning.'

'Good of him to come in.' Turpin fell into step beside her as they left the incident room and made their way down the stairs.

'Good of Sheila to tell him to speak to us,'

said Jan, and smiled before opening the door into the reception area.

A man in his mid-fifties rose to his feet as they entered the room, his greying hair a little on the long side and keen blue eyes that blinked when she shook hands with him before introducing him to Turpin.

'I was going to call, but I figured I had a day off today so it'd be easier to come in,' he said, twisting a folded copy of a daily newspaper between his hands. 'I had to come over to Abingdon with the wife anyway – she wanted to do some shopping, so I thought I'd speak to you.'

'Saves waiting while she wanders around?' said Jan, smiling.

Douglas Jones relaxed, a rueful smile crossing his features. 'With two bookshops in town, it can take a while.'

'Douglas, if you'd like to come through here, we'll get started,' said Turpin, holding open the door through to the interview rooms. 'Do you want a coffee or anything?'

'No, thank you, and please – call me Doug. Everyone else does.'

Jan ignored the recording equipment when she followed the two men into the room and instead pulled out the notebook she had brought with her. Doug Jones wasn't a person of interest in the murder enquiry and so she would type up his statement when she got back to her desk rather than formally record their conversation, enabling her to listen to Turpin and interject if she wanted to clarify anything they were about to discuss.

Once they had got the formalities out of the way and Doug had confirmed his home address and place of work, Turpin launched into his questions.

'As you're aware, we're currently investigating the murder of a teenage boy on Monday night, by the name of Matthew Arkdale,' said the detective sergeant. 'We understand from speaking with Sheila on Wednesday morning that you were working at the train station on Monday morning with her – is that correct?'

'Yes, it is. I start at four o'clock when I'm working a morning shift,' said Doug, settling into his seat and unzipping his waterproof jacket. 'That gives us all time to do the health and safety briefing before the first train arrives.'

'Which platforms were you assigned to?'

'Only platform two that morning – we had a staff member off sick the week before but she was back that day, so I didn't have to split my time between platforms.'

'And Sheila tends to oversee all the platforms?'

'Yes. She was on platform four with Brendan but as station manager she's responsible for all of us.' He shrugged. 'She's a good boss. Likes to wander over and make sure we're all right from time to time, helps out if it's really busy, but then lets us get on with it.'

'And what happened on Monday? Say from about half five, just before the first train arrived?' said Turpin.

'Business as usual, to be honest,' said Doug. He leaned forward, rested an elbow on the table and scratched a stubbly chin. 'Bloody cold that time of day, so I was walking up and down the platform to keep myself moving and take my mind off the temperature. The train from Swindon came in on time – 5.39 – and only a few people got off it. Not surprising at that time of the morning. About half a dozen got onboard and the train left the station a couple of minutes later.'

'Back to the passengers who disembarked,' said Turpin, opening the manila folder under his arm and sliding across a photograph of Matthew. 'Did you notice this teenage boy amongst them?'

Doug swallowed as he took in the boy's closed eyes and deathly pallor. 'Got a grandson about the same age as him. Poor mite.'

'Did you see him on the platform on Monday?'

The man frowned, then passed the photograph back. 'Reckoned I might have done, actually. He was wearing jeans and one of them hooded sweatshirts all the youngsters are wearing these days. There's me in my woolly coat all bundled up against the cold, and him looking like he's off for a stroll in the park.'

Jan turned to a new page of her notebook, her heart rate increasing.

'Doug, this is very important, but did you happen to notice if anyone was travelling with him?'

'No, there wasn't anyone with him. Like I said, only a few people got off the train – maybe three or four, so I think I would've noticed if he was with someone.'

'Did you get the impression that any of those other people might be following him?'

'Not really, no. The rest of them all disappeared pretty quick after the train pulled out of the station – I'd imagine they had jobs to get to, or homes to go to if they'd just finished work somewhere else.'

'And what about Matthew? Did you see what he did?'

'Well, that's the thing you see.' Doug dropped his hands to the table and clasped them together. 'He waited until the train had left, and then wandered over to speak to me.'

'He did?' Jan couldn't keep the surprise from her voice, and shot an apologetic glance at Turpin. 'What did he say?'

'He was asking about the buses. If he could get to Abingdon from there, and how much the fare cost.'

'How did he sound?' said Turpin.

'Young.' Doug managed a sad smile. 'Doesn't seem possible he's dead now. I told him where the ticket office was, pointed him down the stairs and watched him head off. Last thing he said to me was "thanks". That's it.'

'Did he look lost?' said Jan.

'No.' Doug picked at a nail, his eyes troubled. 'If anything, he looked scared.'

CHAPTER TWENTY-SEVEN

Jan climbed from the car, shoved the keys into the outer pocket of her bag and surveyed the properties lining the street.

A row of 1950s-built terraced houses lined the road where she had parked. Chimneys poked up through moss-covered tiles housing television aerials that all pointed south in the vain hope of a signal while satellite dishes fixed to pebble-dashed rendering pointed resolutely in the opposite direction.

She walked past, noting the mixture of privet hedges or low walls constructed from grey cinder blocks and topped with decorative slabs covered in yellowing algae.

A cluster of new houses were being built further along the road, the red brick and sleek roofing tiles a stark contrast to the housing association block of flats she approached.

In fact, the whole neighbourhood appeared to be a mishmash of properties and demographics.

Cursing as her ankle twisted, she looked down to see that the concrete pavers were cracked, with grass and weeds growing between the uneven and chipped surface.

'Which one is it?' she said to Turpin as they drew near.

'Number three. When they turned up, they found the door unlocked. He was on the bathroom floor.'

'Christ. Overdose?'

'We'll soon find out – they couldn't get hold of a local GP at short notice, so they've had to request an ambulance.'

'Who's here with Alice?'

'A probationer – Sam Owen.'

'Hang on,' said Turpin, and paused beside a brick wall that surrounded the driveway into the flats. He pulled out his mobile phone and frowned.

'What's up?' Jan hitched her bag up her shoulder.

He shrugged. 'Missed call. They didn't bother leaving a message, and there's no caller ID.'

'They'll phone you back if it's urgent.'

'Sarge!'

She turned at a shout from the communal doorway that led into the block of flats to see Alice Fields beckoning to them, her face grim.

'This doesn't look good,' he said, before walking over to the constable. 'What's going on?'

'It's Shaun Mansell, Sarge,' said Alice, leading them along a green-tiled hallway and up a flight of stairs. 'The door to his flat was open a crack when we got here. We found him on the bathroom floor.'

She paused at the entry to the flat and gestured inside. 'It's not pretty – looks like he's been there a few days. We've noted life extinct and called for the crime scene investigators to get over here.'

As Jan crossed the threshold and into a narrow hallway, her senses were assaulted with the stench of stale body odour, rotten food and an underlying stink of decay that clung to the walls and ceiling.

To her left she spotted a kitchen, and curled her lip at the overflowing array of chipped crockery in the sink. Discarded takeaway cartons cluttered a narrow worktop, and a greasy sheen coated the cheap linoleum flooring.

'Is that the CSIs?' came a call from beyond an open doorway that led off from the right of the hallway.

Turpin stuck his head around the frame. 'They'll be here any minute, I expect. How're you doing in here?'

'I'll be all right, Sarge,' a male voice answered. 'I don't think this one's going anywhere in a hurry.'

Jan joined him and peered over his shoulder to see a uniformed constable she recognised using his phone to take photographs of a scrawny individual with matted hair who lay sprawled across the tiled floor.

Blood spatter had congealed over the tiles near the man's head, and she covered her nose at the stench of shit and urine that permeated the small room.

'Have you had a chance to speak to the neighbours?'

'Not yet – we'll start as soon as the CSIs get here and we have some more manpower.'

'Fair enough. Any idea what he took?' said Turpin.

'Here,' said Alice. She handed over a sealed evidence bag. 'These had rolled behind the toilet U-bend – Sam here saw them when he was crouching down to take photos before we entered the room. I haven't had a chance to do a proper search around the rest of the flat yet.'

Jan eyed the two yellow pills that slid along the bottom of the bag as Turpin took it from the constable, a jolt of recognition hitting her in the chest as she saw the radioactive trefoil logo stamped on one side. 'They're the same as the ones found in Matthew's pocket.'

'Well spotted, Sam.' Turpin handed back the bag to Alice and beckoned to Jan. 'Let's take a look around.'

She nodded, and pulled out protective gloves from her bag. Handing a set to Turpin, she snapped on her own before making her way through to a living room that on first inspection looked as if it had been last decorated sometime in the 1980s.

Peering over her shoulder at a commotion at the front door, she raised her hand in greeting as Jasper and his team of CSIs donned protective suits and approached the bathroom.

'If you start in here, I'll take the bedroom,' said Turpin, the disgust in his voice evident as his gaze roamed the room. 'God knows what state that's in.'

She smiled. 'Owe you one, Sarge.'

'You do. For Christ's sake look out for needles.'

Jan set her shoulders and began to sift through the rubbish strewn across a two-seater sofa while Turpin's footsteps retreated along the short hallway and then through another door.

She heard him swear profusely as he entered the man's bedroom, and then turned back to the task at hand.

Old newspapers and tobacco packets littered a coffee table, and as she worked her way through the layers of a discarded life using the end of a biro that had been dropped on the stained carpet, she tried to create a sense of Shaun's background.

Correspondence from the housing association and from a local doctor's surgery had been shoved away from one end of the sofa, a trail of food crumbs and stains depicting where the man had sat on a regular basis, the cushions creased and sagging.

The other end of the sofa had been used as a dumping ground for whatever wasn't required and beside the letters, she discovered old receipts from a pharmacy and a repeat prescription for painkillers.

She made a note to phone the doctor's surgery named at the top of the prescription and speak to the man's doctor.

Moving around the room, she continued her search, but found nothing to suggest that anyone else was staying in the flat, or that Shaun Mansell was in possession of any more of the benzodiazepine-based yellow pills that had been found in Matthew's pocket.

She frowned as she made her way back to the hallway, wondering if they were already too late and if Shaun had experimented with the new pills, or whether he had simply dropped them when he collapsed from another medical condition.

Alice Fields stood next to the open front door, relaying a report to Force Control while Sam hovered outside the bathroom.

'Anything?' said Jan, as Turpin emerged from the bedroom.

He shook his head. 'Nothing to suggest that a fourteen-year-old boy was staying here.'

Alice lowered her radio and straightened her vest, then beckoned to them. 'Jasper's taken an initial look, and the funeral directors we use are on their way to move the body.'

'Self-inflicted?' said Turpin, raising an eyebrow as Jasper appeared.

He shrugged. 'Best leave that to the pathologist. If he took something he wasn't used to, then he might not have been expecting the strength – or it might've reacted with whatever else he was taking. I wouldn't want to hazard a guess without seeing a toxicology report. He's got one hell of a whack to the back of his skull, but that could be from where he collapsed onto the bathroom floor.' He peered past Jan to the kitchen, and then to the living room in the other direction. 'The bruising to his arms could be from a multitude of reasons – everything around this place looks like a bloody trip hazard, doesn't it?'

'Okay, thanks anyway,' said Turpin. 'Alice, can you get your colleagues to secure the flat when they get here, and then start interviewing the neighbours? Find out when Shaun was last seen, and whether anyone heard anything suspicious over the past few days.'

'Will do, Sarge.'

Confident that the two uniformed officers could manage the potential crime scene, Turpin shoved his hands in his pockets and led the way back to the car.

'Sounds like our temporary pathologist is going to be working hard this weekend, West.'

Jan snorted. 'Good.'

CHAPTER TWENTY-EIGHT

By Friday afternoon, an air of desperation filled the incident room as the team filed through the door and towards their allocated desks.

Conversations were muted, requests for non-essential paperwork were met with staccato replies, and a weariness had seeped into voices.

Mark ran a hand through his hair, shrugged off his jacket, and wandered over to a spare chair beside Jan as uniformed officers joined suit-wearing detectives and administrative staff in front of the whiteboard.

He lifted his gaze as Kennedy walked out of his office, the detective inspector's expression one of determination, despite the tired faces that turned to face him as he began the briefing.

'Five days, ladies and gentlemen, and we have two dead men we know next to nothing about.' Kennedy ran his gaze over the group. 'I know you're tired. I know you're frustrated, but we cannot afford to let our focus slip. We're at a critical point in this investigation.'

Mark rolled his shoulders, heard Jan shuffle in her seat next to him and watched with bemusement as a tsunami of similar movements swept through the gathered team.

'That's better,' said Kennedy. 'At least it looks like you're awake now.'

A ripple of good-natured responses flitted back and forth, and then the detective inspector held up his hand to silence them.

'First on the agenda – the discovery of our potential suspect, Shaun Mansell, earlier today. Mark, Jan – do you have any more information about his death?'

'I spoke to his GP this afternoon,' said Jan. 'Shaun had been prescribed the painkillers after telling his doctor that over-the-counter ibuprofen was no longer keeping his back spasms at bay.

Apparently it's been an ongoing issue for him since recovering from his car accident three years ago.'

'Was he addicted to them?' said Kennedy.

'Not that the doctor was aware,' said Jan. 'He told me he couldn't see anything noted in the system to that effect. When I asked him whether he knew Shaun was possibly using marijuana to supplement the painkillers, he denied all knowledge and said he works across four clinics on a weekly basis. He said if Shaun didn't venture that information himself or concerns weren't noted during his appointments, then they weren't to know.'

'Covering his arse?' said Alex.

'I reckon he was, yes. He got a bit terse with me after that, and said any other requests for information would have to be made in writing.'

Kennedy added a note to the whiteboard, and then called over to Caroline. 'What about the benefits he was claiming?'

'I spoke to someone at the job centre, guv,' said the detective constable. 'She confirmed that Shaun was claiming a job seeker's allowance that was paid into his bank account every fortnight.'

'When did the local office last see him?'

'Last week, on the Wednesday. The woman I spoke to said he seemed his usual self, and was shocked to hear that he'd been found dead in his flat.'

'Was he claiming for anything else?'

'Not that she could see on her computer,' said Caroline. 'Apparently he was turned down for disability benefit three years ago.'

'Right – thanks, Caroline.' Kennedy gestured to Alex. 'You're next, McClellan – what've you found out about the flat? Who's paying the rent?'

'It's owned by the local housing association, guv.' Alex flipped through his notebook for a moment, found the page he wanted, and then continued. 'I asked when someone last saw Shaun, and he said the annual gas safety check was carried out on the property four months ago. Nothing out of the ordinary was reported by the contractor who did the work. The man I spoke to from the housing association said the rental was due for review in about three months – they were planning to review Shaun's eligibility for it, because they've got five families on their books desperate for housing. As a single bloke, Shaun should've been at the bottom of the list.'

'So, they were just going to evict him?' said Jan, her tone shocked.

Alex shrugged. 'Well, he didn't say that, but…'

'What about next of kin – have they been notified yet?' said Kennedy.

'We spoke to them a couple of hours ago.' Alice Fields rose from her seat at the back so she could be heard. 'His dad owns a construction company out Witney way. Bloody loaded.'

'And he wouldn't help out his son?' said Mark. 'That's harsh.'

'He told us he wouldn't have anything to do with Shaun. Hasn't for years, apparently – even before the car crash and everything.'

'What about his mother?' said Jan.

'Distraught,' said Alice. 'I got the impression she'd been hoping Shaun and his dad could be reconciled. When we left, she told me that they'd been really close when Shaun was a kid, and it was only when he fell in with the wrong crowd after leaving secondary school that things started to go wrong.'

'Did she give you any names?' said Kennedy.

'Only a first name for one of them,' said the police constable, 'and he died four years ago in a farming accident. According to the inquest report, he was operating machinery while under the influence of illegal substances.'

'Has anyone found anything to suggest that Shaun was dealing drugs?' said Kennedy over his shoulder, his pen poised over the whiteboard.

His question was met with silence, and he re-capped the pen before turning to them.

'No? Then why the bloody hell was he found with the same yellow pills that were found in Matthew's pocket? Where are the rest of the bloody things? According to the lab report, his fingerprints were all over that knife. Why kill him?'

'Maybe Shaun was planning to start dealing,' said Jan. 'After all, like Caroline said, he was in danger of losing his free housing within the next few weeks. If he somehow found out that there was a new county lines operation being set up and wanted to get involved at this end, he could've been expecting Matthew to show up.'

'And, maybe they had a falling out when he got here,' said Alex.

Mark ran his gaze over the web of photos and notes that filled the whiteboard, and cleared his throat. 'There is another scenario, guv. If this is the same lot that we were trying to put away in Wiltshire.'

A brief silence followed his words as his colleagues turned to stare at him, and Kennedy leaned against the desk beside the whiteboard.

'Let's hear it, then.'

'The man who stabbed me was killed because they wanted to silence him,' said Mark. 'They couldn't risk him trying to negotiate some sort of deal with us to reduce his sentence in return for information about the whole operation. What if this is the same? What if this gang weren't ready to begin supplying that new drug or Matthew got hold of some samples before the drug had been tested properly? What if, by trying to reach out to me for help, Matthew set in motion a chain of events that the gang are trying to stem by removing the risk of anyone talking?'

Tracy raised her hand. 'Guv? I've had the media relations team on the phone, asking about a statement they want to put out tonight before people start posting things on social media about Shaun Mansell. What should I tell them?'

Kennedy glowered at the floor for a moment, then lifted his chin and glanced over his shoulder at the photograph of Mansell pinned to the whiteboard before turning back to the administrative assistant.

'Tell them we're treating his death as suspicious at this time.'

CHAPTER TWENTY-NINE

The chemical aroma of pine needles and lemon followed Mark around the house as he applied another liberal amount of cleaning foam to the kitchen sink and scrubbed.

A late-nineties indie rock hit blasted from a pair of small speakers on the kitchen worktop, the playlist reminding him of his younger days and normal Friday nights before joining the police as he sang along to the chorus before dropping the cleaning cloth to mimic the guitar solo.

Chuckling under his breath at the thought of what his daughters would say if they could see him, he chucked the cloth into the washing machine and turned his attention to the kitchen bin.

Four nights' worth of takeaway cartons and other rubbish filled the bag, and as he tugged it free from the metal housing, he made a mental note to make a trip to the supermarket in the morning so they would have healthier food over the weekend.

Kennedy had announced the weekend shifts in closing the briefing, and Mark had opted to take the Saturday off so he could relieve Lucy of her extended childminding services.

A surge of helplessness swept through him as he realised neither of his daughters would be children for much longer, and then he smiled at the thought of Louise's horror if she knew he still thought of her as such.

In an hour, he would be having dinner with them on Lucy's boat before arranging a taxi to bring them back home, which was why he was determined to clean the place before he started to walk down to the river.

Tying the ends of the bag together and fishing out the food waste from the bin next to the sink, he made his way out of the back door and over to the wheelie bin. As he slammed shut the lid, he heard his phone ringing from its place next to the speaker and hurried inside, wiping his hands on the cleaning cloth.

The number had been withheld.

'Hello?'

'Turpin? Detective Sergeant Mark Turpin?'

'Yes. Who is this?'

'You should've stayed out of it, Mark. You should've stayed well away.'

'Who is this?'

He frowned, wracking his memory to try to recall if he recognised the voice. It was gruff, used to giving orders, and carried a strong Wiltshire lilt.

He hadn't heard it before.

'How's the family, Mark?'

Anger surged through him, and he tightened his grip on the phone. 'Are you the one who followed Louise home from school?'

'Such a pretty pair, those two. And your wife? Debbie, isn't it? Still talking to her, or is it all over for you two?'

Mark took off for the hallway, and rummaged through his jacket pocket for his work phone.

'Are you listening, Turpin?'

'I'm here. Stay away from them.'

'Pop upstairs a moment, there's a good lad.'

'What?'

'You heard me. Upstairs. Now.'

The command was laced with menace and loathing, and Mark fumbled his work phone before it dropped to the floor.

What was going on?

He climbed the stairs with shaking legs, his left hand gripping the bannister as he held the phone to his right ear.

'Who are you?' he said, hating the tremble in his voice. 'What do you want?'

'You weren't meant to live,' said the man. 'Like a bloody cat with nine lives, you are. What I want is for you to stop poking your nose into things you shouldn't. But here's the thing, Turpin. I don't think you will unless you take me seriously. Go into the spare room. The one you use as an office.'

How does he know?

'Have you been in my house?'

'Lovely things your girls packed to stay with

you,' said the man. 'Shame they're not there at the moment. Walk over to the window.'

Bile rose at the back of Mark's throat as he crossed the room and pulled back the net curtain.

Beyond the tree line, he could see the river.

Moonlight sparkled across the darkened waters, the light fading in and out as the trees swayed in a wind that gusted against the windowpane.

'You can see the boat from there, can't you?' said the man.

'What?'

Through a gap between the houses, he could spot the prow of Lucy's narrowboat silhouetted against the riverbank. His heart lurched as he saw that someone – either Lucy or the girls – had stretched a string of fairy lights along the side since he last looked. The tiny light bulbs twinkled in and out of sight, giving the impression of an impending party or celebration.

His chest ached, a sense that he was out of his depth, out of control.

'Mark? Can you see it?'

'Yes,' he said, louder. 'I can see it.'

'Good. This is what happens when you don't mind your own business.'

The phone went dead.

Mark blinked as seconds later a flash of light appeared from within the narrowboat and then the whole vessel seemed to lift in the air as it burst into flames.

The sound of his screaming echoed off the bedroom walls.

CHAPTER THIRTY

'Mark? Mark – stay on the line. We've got officers, fire engines and ambulances on the way.'

Pain shot through his legs, his footsteps heavy on the concrete pavers, his breathing laboured by the time he ran under the decorative archway of the Guildhall.

The stone gargoyles laughed behind his back from their perches above the walkway as he choked back a sob, his lungs burning.

Kennedy's voice called out from his phone, shoved into his pocket when he had left the house at full pelt, the front door swinging on its hinges.

He could hear more sirens joining the ones

already coming from the direction of the river, and watched as two patrol cars shot past him on Bridge Street.

'Mark? Are you there?'

Gritting his teeth, his panic surging with every step, he crossed the bridge and peered across the waters to where Lucy's boat was moored.

Every breath expelled another grief-stricken cry, every gasp for air drove a piercing agony into his lungs that if he stopped running he knew would escape in a scream.

A fiery orange glow filled the horizon, and as he pushed past worried onlookers who clogged the pavement and hindered his progress, he could hear the crackle and pop of the flames.

Two uniformed officers stood by the metal gate that led to the water meadow, but he recognised neither and glared when the taller of the two raised his hand to prevent him from passing.

'DS Turpin. My daughters are on that boat.'

He didn't wait for the response, didn't acknowledge the astonished look on the constable's face as he tore past and forced a final burst of energy to cross the grass expanse to the river's edge.

Heat fanned his face as he drew closer while a chorus of fearful voices and urgent activity filled the night air.

Other boat owners along the towpath were manoeuvring vessels away from the inferno, as all the while the stench of burning diesel assaulted Mark's nostrils and stung the back of his throat.

He reached the riverbank, panting, his eyes darting left and right, searching among the faces in the crowd that had gathered, their faces stricken.

A tight knot twisted his stomach, a deep pain that made him want to fall to his knees and retch.

Forcing himself to move closer, to keep going, to hold out hope, Mark drew closer to the narrowboat.

He held up his arm to protect his face as a window exploded, showering the riverbank with glass.

The crowd moved back as one, a new terror in their eyes as the scale of the devastation increased.

He spun around at a whoop of sirens to see a

fire engine bumping across the grass towards the river, then turned his attention back to the narrowboat.

Lucy's home.

'Gas explosion,' he heard someone say behind him, and whirled around to see who had spoken, but the woman had turned away and was walking alongside another, hurrying to the safety of a cordon now being established by two more uniformed officers.

It wasn't, he wanted to yell at her.

Instead, he cringed as the fire swept the length of the vessel, unable to see inside.

'Louise! Anna!'

He reached the far end, and slid to a standstill on the loose stones covering the towpath.

The stern was no more – a gaping hole filled with flames had replaced the galley, and smoke was billowing from the roof.

'Sir? Sir – you need to move away.'

He shrugged off the large hand that grasped his shoulder, and turned to face the fireman who had approached him.

'My daughters are on board. My girlfriend, too – and our dog.'

'I'm sorry, sir – you need to move away. It's too dangerous to stand here.'

Mark staggered, the sheer horror of what he was being made to witness too much to bear, his guts threatening to turn to liquid.

'Do something. My daughters…'

His legs gave way as a terrible sound emanated from the hull, then with a groan that punched him in the chest, the vessel started to tilt in the water.

CHAPTER THIRTY-ONE

'Jesus Christ. Fuck, fuck.'

Jan beat the steering wheel with the palm of her hand, and then wrenched it to her right and accelerated past the late-night bus that pulled to the kerb.

'How far away are you?'

'Almost there, guv.'

She could hear the panic in the detective inspector's voice, which did little to allay her worst fears. 'When did he hang up?'

'I lost him after the fire crew told him to move back,' said Kennedy.

'What about his daughters and Lucy?'

'No news yet.'

'Shit. Hang on.'

Jan slewed the wheel left, pulled to a standstill in the council car park and raced over to the footpath. Flashing her warrant card at the uniformed officers at the cordon, she began to run towards the riverbank.

She tried to ignore the stunned and shocked faces of the people who filed past in the opposite direction as they were herded away by other officers, then cried out as her heel caught on the uneven ground.

Gritting her teeth, she craned her neck as she drew closer, trying to find Turpin amongst the first responders and emergency vehicles parked alongside the towpath.

The air was a pungent mix of wood smoke and burnt plastic, spent fuel and chemicals that stung her eyes and throat.

Wiping away tears, she caught sight of a fire officer she had once met at a multi-vehicle accident on the dual carriageway.

The woman raised her hand in greeting before clomping over the grass towards her, her face grim.

'Jan.'

'Where is he, Heather? What happened?'

'Come with me.' The fire officer led the way towards a second cordon that stretched between two liveried patrol cars, ducking under the fluttering tape before pointing at an ambulance. 'Over here.'

Jan dug her fingernails into her palms as they drew closer, and then heard a familiar hacking cough as she rounded the back door of the vehicle.

'Sarge, thank God.'

Turpin sat on the tailgate of the ambulance, a blanket around his shoulders and an arm around each of his daughters.

Anna was in tears, hugging her father so tight that Jan thought he might have bruises the next day, while Louise sat beside him, her face stunned as he stroked her hair.

'Lucy?'

'Here.'

Jan spun around to see the curly-haired artist approaching.

'What happened?'

Lucy shook her head, a fat tear rolling down her cheek. 'It's all gone. Everything.'

'How did you get out?'

'We weren't there.' The woman pushed her curls from her face, and sniffed. 'We'd nipped out to get some garlic bread before Mark arrived.'

'I forgot it earlier,' said Louise. Her voice wobbled. 'If I'd remembered it then... if I'd—'

'Shh,' said Turpin. He gave her shoulders a squeeze. 'You're safe.'

He extricated himself from the two girls, and nodded to a paramedic hovering by the back doors. 'Can you stay with them a minute?'

'Dad?' said Anna.

'I'm not going anywhere. I just need to speak to Jan for a moment. Okay?'

Anna nodded, then curled up beside her sister while the paramedic unfolded an extra blanket and draped it around them.

'I'll wait with them,' said Lucy.

Turpin reached out for her hand. 'You need to hear this, too.'

They moved a few paces away from the ambulance so their voices wouldn't carry on the breeze, and Jan cast her gaze over to the riverbank where the twisted metal frame of the narrowboat poked skywards from the smoking steel hull.

'Jesus, Lucy,' she managed.

Her heart went out to the artist who had made the narrowboat her home for so long.

When she had first seen it, she'd thought the owner might be a hippy, someone who rejected being part of normal society.

Lucy had proved her wrong. The artist was a savvy businesswoman, respected within the community, and her works of art were well renowned.

So, what *had* happened?

As she turned back to Turpin, he pulled the blanket around his shoulders and shivered, and it was at that point she realised that his hair was wet.

'Did you jump in the river?'

'It seemed like a good idea at the time.' He sniffed. 'I couldn't see the girls or Lucy on the towpath amongst the crowd.'

'We got back as they were fishing him out of the water,' said Lucy, and wiped at her eyes before slipping her arm through his. 'Gave me a heart attack. When I saw what had happened to my boat, I thought he went down with it.'

'I got a phone call,' said Turpin, his voice raspy. 'He knew. He knew Anna and Louise were here, and that the girls were staying with Lucy.'

'Who?'

'It has to be the gang leader from Swindon.'

'Did you recognise the voice?'

'I'm not sure. Maybe I heard it once – in passing, but it was a while ago now.'

'What did he say?'

'That I should've stayed out of it.'

'Matthew's murder?'

He nodded.

Jan frowned. 'I wonder why he set fire to the boat if none of you were inside? I mean, one look through the windows and he would've seen it was empty.'

'I always pull the curtains once it gets dark,' said Lucy, and pulled the blanket tighter around her shoulders. 'I've never liked the thought of people being able to see in.'

Turpin squeezed Lucy's shoulder and kissed her hair. 'I never meant to put you in danger.'

'You're alive. We all are.' Lucy forced a smile. 'I'm insured.'

'Still…'

'What do you want to do?' Jan shoved her hands in her pockets so he wouldn't see them trembling. 'Does Kennedy know?'

'Not yet.' He fished out his mobile from his pocket. 'I don't know if it works now that it's been underwater. He'll probably tell me to stay away tomorrow. Perhaps permanently. I would, if I was him.'

Jan swallowed. 'Fucking hell, Mark.'

'Yeah, I know. I'll phone him in a bit. Do me a favour? Keep me posted. I need to get Lucy and the girls back to the house. Uniform have been there to make sure it's safe, and they said the guv has organised a patrol car to stay outside for the next forty-eight hours.'

'Of course, yes.'

They walked back towards the ambulance, Jan wondering what the hell she was going to do to help Turpin as she ran her eyes over his small family.

She stopped in her tracks before they reached the vehicle, her thoughts tumbling.

'Where's Hamish?'

Lucy shook her head and lowered her gaze to her boots.

'They left him on deck when they went into town,' said Turpin.

As her detective sergeant wiped fresh tears from his eyes, she realised the awful truth.

The little dog was missing.

CHAPTER THIRTY-TWO

Dean Evans cradled his bloodied right hand against his stomach, watching with grim satisfaction as a fireball lit the water a quarter of a mile from where he stood, and tried to remember if he'd ever had a tetanus shot.

At least something had gone right tonight.

He raised his eyes to the sky. A sharp wind had turned blustery, scattering the clouds that threatened rain only hours before and now a weak moonlight bobbed in and out of view.

They would have to move fast.

Straining his ears to hear over the rustling

trees and water reeds that crowded the narrowest point of the towpath, he moved forwards from the shadows as a figure approached.

As he drew nearer, Dean could make out the black beanie hat the man had pulled over his salt and pepper hair only a short time ago, his bulky figure dressed in dark jeans and a navy padded jacket.

'Did you see it? Did you see it go up?'

A manic edge crept into the man's voice when he spoke, his words breathless as he took Dean's outstretched hand in a firm grip.

'I did. That'll teach him,' said Dean. 'Did you see him?'

Colin Hadleigh pulled off the beanie, shoved it in his pocket and shook his head. 'Didn't want to hang around. It'd make their day if they got their hands on me after all this time.'

Dean grunted in response.

The Swindon-based drug dealer had a network of places he could stay on a day-to-day basis, the presence of which helped to frustrate the police efforts to arrest him. Time after time, Hadleigh had been so close to being caught, only to step

THE LOST BOY   247

back from the brink – often due to witnesses going missing, or worse.

It was how Hadleigh ran his business – he rarely got involved in the enforcement side of things. That way, the police were left with no evidence.

Everything had been going to plan, except Hadleigh had turned up earlier this afternoon, seemingly willing to risk being caught just because he wanted the satisfaction of seeing Turpin's reaction when he discovered his girlfriend and daughters had perished in the fire.

Dean couldn't talk him out of it, so here he was.

Hadleigh waved his hand at the discarded equipment strewn over the towpath. 'Pack this lot up. I'm dying for a smoke.'

Dean bit back the retort that formed on his lips, then did as he was told.

That was the way it was with Hadleigh. You didn't ask questions, didn't answer back, didn't make demands.

Otherwise you ended up like Shaun Mansell.

He glanced over his shoulder to see Hadleigh

pacing the towpath, his face illuminated by the light from his phone while he blew smoke to one side, his eyes squinting at the screen.

He could have killed for a cigarette, too – to calm his frayed nerves more than anything else – but there was no way he was going to stop and have one.

It would have to wait.

Hadleigh worried him. The man was a good businessman, that much was true, but his temper was unpredictable and dangerous – none more so when he held a grudge.

'What about Turpin?' said Dean, pausing to rub his fingers against his aching back muscles.

Hadleigh chuckled. 'He'll never give up, despite this. Just as well your man Shaun found out where he lives. A shame he tried to threaten me afterwards.'

'First time he'd killed someone, wasn't it?'

'Didn't give him the right to beg from me, and then try blackmail, does it? Like I'd ever risk him going to the police.' Hadleigh dropped the cigarette butt, crushing it into the mud with the toe of his boot. 'No, he needed to be taught a lesson, that one.'

Dean straightened, heaved the black canvas bag over one shoulder, and turned away from the dying glow further downstream. 'We should get out of here, Colin. They'll be looking for us.'

'Us?' Hadleigh spat out the words. 'I doubt they're looking for me. They don't even know I'm here. You're the one who's going to have to stay low for a while, especially after Shaun.'

'But—' A sickening shift in his abdomen twisted Dean's stomach.

'Just for a few days. And don't come back to Swindon. I'll find something else for you to do. Somewhere else.' Hadleigh clapped his hand on his shoulder. 'Now, lead the way.'

The clouds shuffled closer as Dean began to walk, the bag bumping against his ribs with every step.

As the moon blinked in and out between them, a gloom descended on the riverbank. He could make out the lock-keeper's cottage ahead, the brick building's windows darkened on the ground floor while a light shone from an upstairs window.

He said nothing. Hadleigh would have the sense to keep quiet, and so he quickened his step and turned onto the narrow footbridge that crossed the river.

They passed the lock without incident, and he guessed the inhabitants were too intent on watching the scene downstream. No-one called from the cottage, no-one wondering why two men were hurrying away from the towpath at such a late time while a narrowboat burned.

Dean increased his pace, unwilling to push his luck, and hoped the rest of their escape went as well.

He peered over the wire mesh fence that separated the path from the churning waters below, the roar of the current being pushed through the narrow sluice gates beneath his feet.

The metal bridge trembled under the force of the water as he made his way across the river, the weir a stark contrast to the calm of the lock to his rear.

The sound of Hadleigh's footsteps reached him, the man drawing closer when they reached the middle.

'Hey.'

Dean stopped, peered over his shoulder. 'What?'

'What d'you do with the dog?'

'Don't worry about him. He's long gone.'

'Do you want me to carry the bag for a while?' Hadleigh held out his hand and beckoned. 'Come on. Give it here. You've done enough tonight.'

Dean let the strap slide off his shoulder with a sense of relief at losing the heavy weight. 'Are you sure?'

Even he could hear the hope in his voice. It wasn't often Hadleigh offered to help someone, especially when he was the one who employed them.

''Course I am.' Hadleigh's grin contorted his face into a grimace in the fading moonlight. 'Least I can do.'

'Thanks.' Dean handed over the bag and spun to face the path once more, a renewed lightness in his step as he checked his watch.

Another twenty minutes or so, and he could crack open a can of lager, have a cigarette and catch up with the football results on television.

He didn't have time to react when the bag swung into the back of his skull.

The force from the blow pitched him over the

railing and sent him crashing against the concrete weir below where the icy cold water wrapped around him, claiming his last breath before he could cry out.

CHAPTER THIRTY-THREE

When Heather Bankside followed Ewan Kennedy into the incident room on Saturday morning, exhaustion emanated from the fire officer.

She was now wearing her uniform instead of the protective clothing Jan had seen her in the night before and clutched a large tote bag over her shoulder, which she set down on a desk next to the whiteboard before opening it and sliding out a tablet computer. She turned to face the room and ran her gaze over the team at their desks as Kennedy brought her up to date about the investigation in muted tones.

Jan made her way over to the coffee machine,

made enough for herself, Heather and Kennedy and then wandered over, handing out the hot drinks.

'Thanks, Jan,' said Heather. 'I haven't had a chance to have a second one this morning. We didn't finish at the river until three o'clock.'

'Despite that, she's managed to pull together a preliminary report for us,' said Kennedy, 'so if you want to get everyone to gather round, we'll get the briefing started.'

Five minutes later, Jan and her colleagues sat in a semicircle of chairs in front of the whiteboard, falling silent as the DI began.

After making a formal introduction about Heather and her work, Kennedy moved to one side and let the fire officer continue.

'As you can imagine, for those of you who weren't on scene last night, there was a substantial amount of damage to the narrowboat once we got the fire out. This was exacerbated by the nature of the boat – in a small space like that, with the amount of chemicals on board that the owner used for her art, together with other materials and soft furnishings – it didn't take long for the flames to take hold. Together with the location of the mooring, and the difficulties in getting our equipment to the riverbank, we were unable to save it.'

Heather paused, and took a sip of coffee before continuing. 'What we have managed to ascertain is that the fire wasn't caused by a gas leak.'

'With a fire like that, how come the boat didn't sink completely?' said Alex.

'The hull is constructed from steel,' said Heather. 'We can see extensive damage to the cabin area, but for the most part the hull withstood the brunt of the fire. The heat from the fire was directed through the weaker parts of the boat, namely the cabin and roof.'

'Mark said he received a phone call minutes before the fire telling him to look out his window towards the boat,' said Kennedy. 'This was a targeted attack, not an accident.'

'I realise that,' said Heather. 'But at the moment, we haven't found anything to support an arson theory. Once we have the boat out of the water, we can reassess it.'

'If Mark and his family were targeted, then

wouldn't there be signs of a break-in?' said Caroline.

'We'll continue working our way through the boat this afternoon,' said Heather. 'Of course, we'll be looking for evidence to support that and we'll let you know what we find.'

'There was a dog on board,' said Jan. 'Hamish. Surely, he would have seen off an intruder or at least made enough noise that the boat owners along that stretch of river would have been alerted?'

Kennedy turned to her, his eyes troubled. 'If whoever did this knew that Mark's family were on board the boat, and not with him, then it stands to reason they knew there was a dog on board. They might've dealt with Hamish first so he didn't alert the neighbours.'

'Have any of your officers on scene found the dog?' said Heather.

'No. Nor have they found a body.'

'All right. I'll let my team know in case we find his remains on the boat. If we do, maybe it will help you get some answers.'

Kennedy thanked the fire officer, and then dismissed the team.

Jan flipped shut her notebook, frustrated.

Two men dead, Turpin's family lucky to be alive and dealing with the loss of their beloved dog, and they were no closer to finding out who was responsible.

'It's going to be a long day,' muttered Caroline as they walked back to their desks.

'No shit.'

CHAPTER THIRTY-FOUR

'Any news?' said Turpin.

Jan locked her computer screen and wandered over to the window, peering through the blinds at a grey sky that lingered over the police station car park.

'Heather gave us her initial findings earlier.'

'And?'

Jan sighed, let the blinds snap back into place, and leaned against the wall. 'They haven't found anything to support a theory of arson yet, Sarge.'

'That's bullshit. Even I could smell the petrol. It's arson, Jan.'

'Well, Heather did say that was only the

preliminary findings.' Jan could hear the defensive tone in her voice, and bit her lip. 'There were all the other chemicals on board from Lucy's painting, too, remember. I suppose they have to work their way through the whole lot before they can give us something conclusive.'

'So, what did Kennedy say?'

'Told her to keep us up to date as they're sifting through the wreckage. They've got a crane down there now, lifting it out of the water.'

'I know. I'm watching it from the bedroom window.'

'How are you holding up?'

Turpin sighed. 'Not good. We're all missing Hamish, and then there's the thought that they could've so easily have been on board when it happened. It hit Lucy hard this morning when she realised she hasn't got a home to go to. I mean, yes, she's insured but it's all the memories she had on the boat – mementoes that belonged to her grandmother, things like that.'

'One theory going around is that whoever did this might've done something to Hamish before the fire. To stop him from barking to alert Lucy's neighbours. Our suspect – when we find him –

must've been watching them prior to the fire to know that there was a dog on board that could raise the alarm.'

'Christ. I don't know what's worse. Thinking he died in the fire, or that someone hurt him beforehand.'

'I'm sorry. Any more thoughts on who phoned you?'

'I didn't sleep because all I could hear was his voice in my head, but I can't think of a name. We never got close to who was running the gang in Swindon – that all went tits up after our informant was killed.'

'Kennedy's in touch with Wiltshire Police,' said Jan. 'There's a meeting with them at four o'clock via video conference – apparently, the Chief Super's attending.'

'Bugger. I was thinking of coming in. Best I don't if they're both there.'

'You're better off staying with Anna and Louise for now. Don't worry, I'll phone you—' She broke off as Caroline walked into the incident room and beckoned to her. 'I've got to go – we were waiting for the post mortem to be completed on Shaun Mansell, and Caroline and Alex have just got back from the morgue.'

'Let me know what they say?'

'Will do.' She ended the call and then hurried over to where the team congregated around the whiteboard, sliding onto a seat beside Alex. 'Okay?'

He nodded, although his face remained pale. 'I thought you said it got easier over time.'

'Did I?'

'Okay, quiet everyone.' Kennedy strode to the front of the group. 'Caroline, do you want to get up here and give us a summary of what Ferguson had to say for himself?'

The detective constable weaved past her colleagues, and turned her notebook back a few pages before speaking in a clear voice that rang out across the room.

'According to his findings, Ferguson will state in his report that Shaun Mansell was still breathing last weekend. He estimates that Shaun died either on the Monday or Tuesday from an overdose of benzodiazepines and painkillers.'

'Accidental, or otherwise?' said Jan.

'Otherwise, according to Ferguson,' said Caroline.

Kennedy held up his hand. 'Hang on – Tom? Can you chase up the CCTV footage for the streets around Shaun's flat and see whether you can spot him? Start on Saturday and work your way forward so we can get a feel for his movements leading up to his death.'

'Will do, guv.'

'Sorry, Caroline – you were saying?'

'Ferguson also found a lot of undigested alcohol in Shaun's stomach contents – whisky. On top of the painkillers he was already being prescribed and the pills he took, it was a lethal combination.'

'I didn't see anything to suggest he was a heavy drinker when we were at his flat. There were no empty bottles or open ones lying around,' said Jan. 'If he was taking painkillers on top of drinking alcohol, it could've been fatal, couldn't it? Even before we take into account the benzodiazepines, I mean.'

'How fast can we get the toxicology results to support the theory of an overdose?' said Kennedy.

'I'll keep on top of it, but they're not in until

Monday morning.' Caroline frowned, and then re-read her notes. 'Ferguson did say something this morning that didn't make sense to me at the time. He told us that one of Shaun's front teeth was chipped, and the damage looked recent. I thought maybe he meant Shaun might've knocked it when he fell to the floor, but what if he was made to drink the whisky? Someone forcing a bottle to his lips might've chipped a tooth.'

'Jasper's been through that flat and there's no mention of a discarded whisky bottle in his report.' The DI picked up the phone on Tracy's desk, pressed the speed dial and then held up his hand to silence the team as the call was answered. 'Steph? It's Ewan Kennedy downstairs – could you get a uniform patrol back to the flats where Shaun Mansell lived? Give them a heads up that they're going to have to go through the communal bins at the back of the property – we need to find a whisky bottle.'

He thanked the Control operator, and then dropped the phone back into its cradle before barking out orders.

'Tom – add to your team's task list to keep an eye out on that CCTV footage for anyone acting suspiciously around Shaun's flat. Jan and Caroline – I want you to review the neighbours' statements, then re-interview them today to find out if anyone heard any signs of a struggle in Shaun's flat, or whether they spoke with him prior to his estimated time of death. You can liaise with uniform about the search through the bins while you're there.'

Kennedy flicked through the current action list that had been generated from the database. 'Alex, I want you to work with me on the call Mark said he received last night prior to the narrowboat catching fire. Jan brought in his mobile phone this morning – it's worse for wear after being in the river – but if we can't pull anything useful from it then we'll hand it over to the digital forensics team. The rest of you I want manning the phones in case we receive any new information so we can take action straight away.'

He peered over his glasses before waving them away.

'Dismissed.'

CHAPTER THIRTY-FIVE

Optimistic sunlight broke through the morning cloud cover as Mark, Lucy and the girls walked along the riverbank.

The sky overhead was at odds with the thoughts that pummelled Mark's mind as they drew closer to where Lucy's narrowboat had been moored. He squeezed her hand as they approached the first of the boats that had been moved away from the inferno the previous night, and nodded to the familiar face that appeared at a cabin window before the owner came out on deck.

'If there's anything you need, Lucy, you've

got my phone number. Just let me know,' said the woman.

'I will, thank you,' said Lucy.

'We all want to help. I can't imagine what you're going through.'

Lucy nodded, and Mark felt her hand tighten in his as they moved away.

He lifted his gaze to the horizon, running his eyes over the line of trees that bordered the river. He knew his search was in vain – Hamish had either perished in the fire or, according to his colleagues' theories, been dispatched by the arsonist so that he could approach the narrowboat without the dog raising the alarm.

He clenched his jaw.

As one, the small group stopped when they drew closer to the narrowboat's old mooring.

The ground had been churned up by heavy boots, emergency vehicles and, finally, the crane used to drag the boat's skeleton from the water. Remnants of grass gave way to mud across the river bank and down to the water, leaving scorched and singed reeds as the only evidence of last night's fire.

Across the water on the other side, dog

walkers craned their necks and pointed to the space where Lucy's home had been. The colourful painted narrowboat with its wind chimes, flowerpots and quirky bric-à-brac had been a familiar sight for many.

A short man wearing a padded jacket and clutching a clipboard stood a few steps from the water's edge, his head bowed as he worked.

'It's Tony, from the insurance brokers,' said Lucy. 'I wasn't sure if he'd come out today.'

She introduced Mark, before he made his excuses and wandered back to the first boat, after making sure that Anna and Louise stayed away from the slippery water's edge.

The woman had her back to him while she used a cleaning spray and a cloth to wipe down the windows of her boat, and glanced over her shoulder as he approached.

He held out his hand. 'I'm sorry, we haven't been formally introduced. I'm DS Mark Turpin.'

She put down the cleaning spray. 'Wendy Keller.'

'I've not seen you before, have I?'

Wendy shook her head. 'We usually spend the warmer months pottering around the Midlands.

This is our winter mooring, although last year we had the opportunity to stay at a friend's house in the south of France.' She managed a smile. 'Wasn't going to turn that down.'

'I don't blame you. I used to rent a boat along here, last summer. It didn't have any heating – I couldn't wait to get out before the cold weather set in.' He checked over his shoulder to see Anna and Louise talking to another boat owner further up the riverbank, the couple hugging Louise and pointing further upstream.

'They're lovely girls, as is Lucy.' Wendy twisted the cleaning cloth in her hand. 'I can't believe what's happened. Thank God they weren't hurt.'

'I don't suppose you know anything about our dog, do you? He hasn't been seen since the fire.'

The woman's face fell. 'No, I haven't seen him. That's terrible. I'm so sorry to hear that. We used to love having him come to visit us.'

Mark cleared his throat. 'I'm going to have to ask in an official capacity, Wendy – did you see or hear anything last night out here on the towpath before her boat caught fire?'

'Like what?' The woman's eyes widened.

'I don't know. Perhaps someone hanging around who you didn't recognise. Anything that sounded suspicious.'

'No, can't say I did, and David – my husband – never mentioned anything.'

'When did you first realise something was wrong?'

'The wind must've changed direction, because a few moments before the boat caught fire, David said he could smell smoke. That's always a worry, obviously. We went out on deck. We were moored here, so when we saw the fire, we – I'm sorry.' She broke off and wiped at her tears. 'It was such a shock. To see that happen. We put on our boots and rushed along to the mooring, and by then the two boat owners closest to hers were casting off and moving away as fast as they could while the rest of us got what buckets and things we could and started trying to put out the flames.'

'That was incredibly dangerous,' said Mark. 'Weren't you worried about the windows exploding?'

Wendy shook her head. 'We were frightened, yes, but we thought Lucy and your girls were in there. We had to do something.'

Mark reached out and squeezed her arm, his throat aching. 'Thank you.'

'We stick together, those of us who live on the water,' she said. 'You'd have done the same for us.'

'I would, yes.'

'There you go, then.' The woman sniffed. 'We were so relieved when they turned up at the same time the police and fire crews got here. Poor Hamish, though.'

'I know.'

'Dad!'

He turned at Anna's shout to see his youngest daughter beckoning to him.

'You should be with them,' said Wendy. 'I'll mention to David that you were here – he's in town at the moment, but if he remembers anything about last night, I'll tell him to let you know.'

'Thanks,' said Mark.

He handed over one of his business cards before hurrying along the towpath to where Lucy stood next to Anna and Louise beside another boat owner he recognised.

'James.'

'Mark.' The older man scratched at his beard

and then gestured to Lucy. 'I was just saying, a bunch of us have started a collection to raise some money towards getting this one back on her feet.'

'I told him he didn't have to do that,' said Lucy, blushing.

'Don't be daft, lass. Not after everything you've done for us over the years.' James's eyes reddened under bushy eyebrows. 'You're like a daughter to us, y'see. That insurance lot will only pay out so much. You're going to need some help, so don't try to stop us.'

'He's right, you know,' said Mark. 'We're only going to be able to do so much ourselves.'

Anna tugged on his coat sleeve. 'James saw someone with Hamish last night.'

'Did you?' He tried to batten down the hope, but it was there in his voice for all to hear. 'Where?'

'Walked straight past here,' said James. 'With him on a lead.'

'What?'

'I thought maybe Lucy had friends over and one of them was taking him for a stroll to stretch his legs before it got too late.'

'But we never walk him on a lead along here.'

James shrugged. 'I didn't think much about it at the time, but when Lucy said your girls were over last night, I wondered what other guests she might have. It wasn't a big boat, was it?'

'Can you describe the man you saw?'

'Not really. It was so dark, see? I'd only stuck my head out the door to empty the bin before going to bed, and I saw them at the end of the towpath over there, heading towards the lock. I didn't recognise him, but I'd know Hamish a mile off. Mind you, he didn't seem happy about it. I thought he was tugging on his lead a bit, to be honest. Come to think of it, maybe it was just a piece of rope. Hard to tell. The bloke sounded impatient with him – I figured he was just wanting him to hurry up and do his business before taking him back to Lucy's.' James shrugged, a sorrowful expression crossing his weather-beaten face. 'Sorry, lass. I just assumed he was a friend of yours.'

Mark said nothing, and reached into his pocket as his phone began to ring. He took one look at the number, and grimaced. 'I have to take this.'

He answered the call and turned away.

'Debbie – how's things? I tried to call a couple of days ago, but it went straight through to voicemail.'

'Lousy phone signal,' said his ex-wife. 'How's everything there?'

Mark crossed his fingers behind his back, took a deep breath, and then forced a smile on his face so it would reach his voice.

'Busy.'

'You sound tired.'

'Just work, that's all – something cropped up. Lucy's been helping with the girls, taking them out to museums and things like that, so they haven't been bored.'

'Well, I'll see you on Tuesday – you can all tell me your news when I see you.'

'You're coming back already?'

'Mum's improved a lot, and my cousin Charlotte is flying over to be with her for a couple of weeks to get her settled back into her own routine. Gillian and I will go back after that for a bit, you know – taking turns. Hopefully it won't be for long. Anyway, I'll fill you in on the details next week. My flight lands on Tuesday morning so I'll pop over in the afternoon, if that's okay?'

'Give me a call when you land, will you?'

'Something the matter?'

Debbie's voice became tinged with concern, and Mark turned to see his daughters watching, their expressions doubtful. He swallowed. 'I'll tell you when I see you, all right? Not over the phone.'

After assuring her that both girls were well, Mark ended the call and shoved the phone into his pocket, then turned around to see Lucy shaking her head.

'You're going to be in the shit when she gets back.'

'I know.'

CHAPTER THIRTY-SIX

A sickening aroma of dirt and decay hit Jan in the face when the uniformed constable beside her lifted the lid of the industrial-sized rubbish bin.

As one, the gathered officers reared back, recoiling from the stench that emanated from the overflowing container.

'What day is bin day?' said Jan, holding her arm in front of her face, protective gloves covering her hands.

'The residential collections are done on a Tuesday,' said Caroline. She wrinkled her nose as she cast her gaze across the rubbish shoved into the bin by the residents of the flats above. Her eyes opened wide at a scurrying scratching sound. 'Fucking hell, is that a rat? I hate rats.'

'Think of it as a giant gerbil.' PC Nathan Willis winked. 'Not as cute, though.'

Jan narrowed her eyes at him. 'In that case, we'll leave you to it.'

He groaned, then beckoned his colleagues closer and they began to sift through the discarded remnants of the residents' lives.

Jan snapped off her gloves and hurried away from the bin, inhaling the fresher air in the middle of the communal area behind the flats before turning to watch the team work.

'If the bins aren't collected until Tuesday, that whisky bottle could be right at the bottom, according to the timeline Ferguson gave us,' said Caroline.

'If it's in there.' Jan dropped her gloves into a biohazard bin set next to the back wheel of one of the patrol cars, pulled a small bottle of antiseptic hand gel from her bag, then grimaced as she smeared it over her hands. 'They're going to be here a while. Let's go and have a chat with Shaun's neighbour while we're waiting. What's his name?'

Her colleague took the proffered hand gel. 'Thanks – Frank Tyler. He's lived here for five years, according to the statement uniform took last week.'

Jan dropped the bottle back into her bag and followed Caroline through the back door into the block of flats. 'Anything useful?'

'Not at the time, but perhaps if we mention that Shaun might have had someone visit him who was older than Matthew, it might jog his memory. Last week, we were only looking for Matthew, right? Not another bloke.'

'True. All right, lead the way.'

She fell into step behind Caroline as they took the stairs to the second floor, pausing for a moment on the landing to check their notes before making their way to the door of flat number four.

Ringing the door bell, she waited for a moment and, when no footsteps approached, rapped her knuckles against the wooden surface.

'Maybe he's not in?' said Caroline.

Jan held up her hand at the sound of movement the other side, and then the door was wrenched open.

A ruddy face peered across a brass security

chain at her. 'What do you want? I don't vote anymore and if you're selling something, you can bugger off.'

Caroline reached for her warrant card at the same time as Jan. 'Mind if we have a word, Mr Tyler? It's about your neighbour, Shaun Mansell.'

'Have they let out his flat to someone else yet? Perhaps a young woman this time – that'd be an improvement.' He leered at them, pale blue eyes flicking to the door opposite. 'Mind you, anything'd be an improvement on Shaun. Lazy bastard.'

'Can we come in, Mr Tyler? Perhaps continue this conversation without the security measures?' said Jan, biting back her disgust.

'I suppose so.'

He rolled his eyes, released the chain from the door and held it open, ogling Caroline as she walked past.

'After you, Mr Tyler.'

Jan smirked as he slammed the door shut before leading the way through to a flat mirroring the layout of Shaun Mansell's across the hallway.

A television screen blared from a corner of the living room and a yellowing fog of cigarette smoke hung in the air while Tyler slouched across to a threadbare armchair and sank into it, twisting a butt into a full ashtray.

'Could you turn the telly down?' said Jan, forcing a smile. 'We might be able to hear ourselves talk.'

Tyler's lip curled, but he reached out for the remote and jabbed a finger at it.

The screen darkened.

'I've already told the coppers that were here the other day everything I know.'

'We've received new information that we're following up,' said Caroline, ignoring the man's stare and moving to the window. 'Your flat overlooks the bins downstairs.'

'So?'

'Did you hear anyone visiting Shaun Mansell between Saturday and Thursday last week?'

'Don't think so. Already told the others that.'

Jan bit back a sigh. If the man's television was blasting out on a daily basis like it had been when they had arrived, she wasn't surprised he missed anything going on outside his front door.

'What about hearing an argument?' she said. 'Perhaps shouting?'

'No.'

She heard it then.

A tremble, ever so subtle, but it was there.

'Frank? Has someone threatened you?'

He shook his head, and then dropped his gaze to his lap, his mouth downturned.

'Did you see something?'

The man exhaled, a sigh that made his shoulders sag as if all the energy was leaving his body.

'Tuesday night. I heard a shout, and then something heavy fell over. I turned down the telly, but it had all gone quiet.'

'And was the sound coming from Shaun's flat?'

'Yes. I got up and peeked through the gap in the front door. A man came out of the flat. He didn't see me at first. I think I made him jump.'

'What did he do?'

'I-I asked him if everything was all right. He said Shaun had asked him to go out and buy some more baccy, and did I know where the nearest shop was. I figured they were just smoking some of that dope I could always smell whenever Shaun opened the door, so I told him about the petrol station up the road that was probably still open.'

'What time was that?' said Caroline.

'About half past ten, quarter to eleven, I reckon.'

'Did he say anything else?' Jan edged closer, holding her breath to avoid inhaling the man's body odour, rather than from a sense of anticipation.

'Told me thanks, and then headed off down the stairwell.'

'Was he alone?'

'Yes.' Tyler frowned. 'There's one other thing – he had his hand inside his jacket. Like he was holding something underneath it, do you know what I mean?'

'Did you check Shaun's front door?'

Tyler shook his head, and shuddered. 'I didn't want to. I didn't want to know.'

'Did you hear anything outside, after the man left?' said Caroline, and jerked her thumb over her shoulder towards the window.

'I'm not sure. No.'

Jan leaned back as her mobile phone began to ring, and fished it from her bag. 'DC West.'

'It's Nathan downstairs. We've found a whisky bottle – there's traces of blood just inside the neck of it.'

'We're on our way.' Ending the call, she stood and shoved the phone away. 'Mr Tyler, we'll send up a couple of our colleagues to take an updated statement from you. I'll also arrange for a sketch artist to visit – I'd appreciate it if you'd give him a description of the man you saw.'

'Will it help?'

'I hope so, yes.'

'All right, then.'

Tyler shuffled and began to raise himself from the armchair.

'No need to see us out.' Jan waved him back. 'Thanks for your time.'

'Will I be safe here?'

His voice rang out as they reached the door.

Caroline pursed her lips, and then turned back. 'Do you have someone you can call, family or something like that?'

'No.'

'We'll have our colleagues give you the phone number for a locksmith,' she said, a note of apology in her voice. 'I can't promise that we can provide protection at this time, but it'd be worth getting someone to have a look at that front door lock at least.'

Jan led the way back downstairs, and peered up at the window to Tyler's flat as they hurried towards the now empty industrial bin.

The man stared down at them, his eyebrows knitted together as he watched the police officers going through the other bins.

'Do you think he saw Shaun's killer?' said Caroline, following her gaze.

'I do, yes. And I think Mr Tyler is lucky to be alive. Whoever murdered Shaun seems to be doing his best to cover his tracks, doesn't he?'

CHAPTER THIRTY-SEVEN

'I didn't expect to see you for a few more days. What are you doing here on a Sunday morning?'

Mark held open the door for Louise and Anna, then turned to Tom Wilcox who leaned on the reception desk, a look of intrigue in his eyes.

'Change of plans. Can you give these two some visitor passes before I show them through to the atrium?'

'Sure. Does Kennedy know you're here?'

'Not yet.'

Wilcox pursed his lips. He showed Louise and then Anna where to stand while photos were taken of them before he handed over the passes. 'And how are you two?'

Anna shrugged, and slipped her hand into Mark's.

'Are you going to help Dad catch who did this?' said Louise. She jutted out her chin at the police sergeant.

'I am, yes. We all are.'

'Good.'

'Thanks, Tom.' Mark guided his daughters through the secure inner door before leading them through to the atrium. He pulled out his wallet and gave Louise his debit card. 'You'll need it for the vending machine. The TV remote is there – don't let Alex get his hands on it during his break, otherwise you'll end up watching house renovation programmes.'

Anna took it from him and wandered over to one of the chairs under the television.

'Dad?' Louise waited until her sister was busy flicking through the channels before turning to him. 'Are you okay? I mean, everyone keeps asking us and Lucy how we are, but no-one asks you, do they?'

He didn't know what to say, and instead pulled her into a hug. 'Thanks.'

'You didn't answer the question.' After a moment, she extricated herself and stared at him. 'Are you? Okay, I mean.'

'I'm angry. Frustrated we haven't found who killed Matthew, and I'm pissed off that you, Anna, and Lucy have been targeted.'

'Are you scared?'

Mark blinked, taken aback by his daughter's maturity and her concern.

Her gaze didn't waver.

'A bit, yes,' he said, 'but that's why I wanted to come here. To help.'

A sad smile flickered across her lips. 'You'd have driven us up the wall if you'd stayed at the house.'

'Was I that obvious?'

'Very.'

He glanced over his shoulder, then back to her. 'I have to go. DI Kennedy will be starting the morning briefing in a moment, and I want to be there for that.'

Louise waved her phone at him. 'What do I say if Mum calls?'

'I'll leave that up to you.'

'Have you told her?'

'Not yet.'

'You're going to be in *so* much trouble.'

'Yeah, Lucy said something to that effect.'

He gave her a gentle shove towards her sister, then made his way through the building and up the stairs to the first floor.

Kennedy was midway through his introductory pep talk when Mark entered the incident room. He peered over his reading glasses, lowering his notes.

'What the bloody hell are you doing here, Turpin?' he barked.

'Helping, guv.' Mark dropped his backpack onto his chair, pulled out his notebook, and wandered across to where the rest of the team had gathered.

Jan kicked out a chair from under the desk she leaned against, the wheels butting against Mark's shoe as he stopped it rolling and nodded his thanks before sitting.

Kennedy glared at him, then turned his attention back to the assembled team.

'As I was saying, we're expecting a further

update from Heather about her team's findings regarding the fire in the next day or so. Moving on to Shaun Mansell – Alice, how are you getting on with the CCTV?'

The police constable stepped forward and faced her colleagues. 'We started by taking a look at footage along the road outside the flats between Monday morning and Friday afternoon when Shaun was found dead. That timeframe was based on the pathologist believing Shaun was still alive last weekend. In fact, we can corroborate his report because we do have images of Shaun outside a block of flats further up the street late Sunday afternoon. He was facing the direction of his flat when the camera caught him there.'

'What about Monday?' said Alex.

'That's where we've got more work to do,' said Alice. 'There's no sign of Shaun during the morning, but in the afternoon we've got someone entering the street at the junction with the main road who's made some effort to hide his features.' She nodded to Tracy, who handed out copies of a video still image. 'As you can see from this, he's wearing a plain baseball cap and his collar up, and there are no distinguishing features we can use to track his movements after he leaves the area.'

'What happens when he gets to Shaun's flat?' said Mark, peering at the photograph Jan held.

Alice sighed. 'That's what I meant about having more work to do. There was a removals truck parked at the kerb in front of the camera closest to Shaun's flat, so we lose sight of this person as he walks behind it. We can't be sure whether he went to Shaun's flat or walked up an alleyway that runs alongside a neighbouring property. I've had a chat with Tom, and we plan to head back there this morning to speak to the people who were moving out to find out if they saw this person. We'll also interview property owners whose gardens back onto the alleyway to see if they saw anyone acting suspiciously.'

'What about the removals company?' said Jan. 'Their logo is easy to see on these images.'

'Closed until the morning,' said Alice. 'We'll get in touch with them first thing and arrange to interview the men who are pictured here as soon as possible.'

'That's good work, constable,' said Kennedy, ignoring the wave of frustration that flitted

through the team as the police constable returned
to her seat. 'Keep me updated about anything
useful you find out. Jan – what's happening about
the whisky bottle found in the bin yesterday?'

'It's been sent off so the blood on it can be
compared with Shaun's.'

'And you say his neighbour reckons he saw
someone leaving the flat on Tuesday night?'

'Yes, guv. Frank Tyler. I've had uniform take
an updated statement from him, and he's working
with a sketch artist to give us an idea of what the
bloke looked like. I should have that sometime
this afternoon so I can put it into the system. I'll
email everyone once that's done.'

'Thanks. Did Tyler mention whether he saw
anyone else enter or leave the flat?'

'He didn't,' said Jan, 'but I'm wondering
whether his killer was staying there prior to
murdering him. I mean, just because Shaun's
fingerprints were on the knife used to kill
Matthew doesn't mean he was responsible, now
does it?'

'I'm inclined to agree.' Mark leaned forward
in his seat. 'What if the knife that was found with

Shaun's fingerprints on it was removed from his flat by this bloke Frank Tyler saw?'

'Then why kill Shaun as well?' said Jan.

'Because whoever did this is cleaning house,' said Mark. 'It's what happened on the case I was working on in Swindon. As soon as he thought he was threatened – in our case, it was because of an informant's cover being blown – he started getting rid of anyone who might say something. The man who killed our informant and tried to kill me was murdered while he was on remand. It's why that investigation stalled.'

Kennedy slipped off his reading glasses and rubbed the bridge of his nose. 'What made him panic, though? Matthew coming here?'

'It's possible,' said Mark. 'I mean, we *think* Matthew came here to find me. What I don't understand is why Lucy's boat was destroyed. If whoever is doing this wants me dead, why didn't he come to my home?'

'Sarge?'

A voice from the other side of the group made him look away from the DI.

Caroline sat with her laptop open and shook

her head, a sad smile on her lips. 'A few months ago it was all over the news, remember?'

She flipped around the laptop so he and Kennedy could see the screen. Plastered across it was a news headline.

Newly assigned detective awash with success.

Mark groaned, his shoulders sagging.

He remembered the piece – a reporter had turned up with a photographer after the team had put away a serial killer targeting parish priests. Wanting to show Mark in the most picturesque surroundings to appeal to a wider audience – the reporter deeming the outside of the police station "too political" – the journalist had seized upon the discovery that Mark was renting a narrowboat.

One look at the peeling paint and rundown vessel was enough for the photographer to suggest they pose Mark along the bank with Lucy's prettier narrowboat as a backdrop.

'What about the phone call I got? Any luck tracing a number?'

Jan shook her head. 'Nothing yet, Sarge. We've passed it on to digital forensics. They did find out that it was purchased from a shop based in Swindon, but there's been no activity on it since that call to you. They'll let us know if they find out more.'

With that, Kennedy brought the briefing to a close, and beckoned to Mark and Jan. 'My office, now.'

He led the way across the incident room, and then closed the door while they sat in the chairs opposite his desk.

'Have you spoken to your ex-wife?'

'This morning, guv.'

'How did she take the news?'

Mark glanced at Jan, then back to the detective inspector. 'I didn't tell her, guv. She can't get back here until Tuesday, her mother has been seriously ill, and I didn't want to have that conversation over the phone.'

'Are you sure that's wise?'

'I'm not sure about anything anymore, guv.'

Kennedy wrinkled his nose, opened his mouth to retort, then seemed to think better of it and slid a manila folder across the desk, tapping his finger on the rough cardboard surface.

'We've managed to call in some favours,' he said. 'From tomorrow, you and your family will be staying at a property on the outskirts of town so don't make any plans to come here in the morning. You'll be picked up from home by an unmarked car, and taken to the house. Pack what you need for a two-week stay, just in case.'

'Wait – what? A safe house?' Mark looked from Kennedy to Jan, astounded. 'I need to be here. I mean, by all means, have the girls there – Debbie, too when she gets back from St Helier, but I can't. We need to stop whoever's doing this.'

'Leave that to us.' Kennedy strode to his desk and picked up a pen. 'Which flight is Debbie coming back on?'

'The half seven flight into Gatwick on Tuesday morning.'

'We'll have someone meet her at the airport and bring her straight here. Is Gillian with her?'

'Yes.'

'All right, we'll arrange to take her home. I don't think she's in danger, but we'll have a patrol monitoring her house as well.'

'It won't work.' Mark dug his fingernails into the soft arms of the chair. 'The safe house, I mean.'

'I'm not putting you at risk,' said Kennedy. 'We've already got a young kid and a man dead, not to mention your informant in Swindon and the man who tried to kill you there.'

'I've got to be seen to be working by whoever's behind all of this, otherwise he'll suspect something's wrong. There's no other way.'

'It's not negotiable.'

Mark pushed himself out of the chair and began to pace the carpet.

He had to stay involved – he had to know what progress the investigation was making, and what direction it was taking.

More importantly, he had find out who was responsible for the killings while attempting to launch a potent cocktail of benzodiazepine-type drugs to unsuspecting addicts within the community.

He paused. 'What if we use this business of me going to a safe house as a way to draw him out?'

'What do you mean?' said Jan.

'Make it look as if my family are planning to remain with me at my house, but move them under cover of darkness while you're watching the street. Take them to this safe location you've organised. Meanwhile, I can make sure I'm seen. It'll be too enticing for whoever is responsible for all of this to resist. If we draw him out rather than waiting for him to strike, we can arrest him. We're working blind here at the moment – we don't even know what he looks like, where he's been, or where he's staying now that Shaun Mansell is dead.'

Kennedy looked troubled. 'It's a hell of a risk, and I'd have to run it past the Chief Superintendent first.'

'Then do it, please, guv.'

'It's too dangerous,' said Jan. 'You can't.'

'I have to,' said Mark. 'Whoever is doing this isn't going to give up until he's finished, or I'm dead.'

CHAPTER THIRTY-EIGHT

Jan shoved her hands in her pockets, her boots kicking up early morning dew from the grass that led down from the picturesque Abbey Gardens to the riverbank.

In front of her, Caroline set a fast pace towards a muddy beach area forming a crescent-shaped space that was crawling with police divers and uniformed officers.

The stench of rotting vegetation and damp undergrowth reached her as they drew nearer.

Sirens bleated in the distance, the sound wavering as the wind snatched it away for a moment, before returning with a renewed urgency as she followed her colleague.

A fine mist covered the surface of the water, a froth forming that churned at the base of the waterfall and trapped litter, thin tree branches, and other remnants of greenery before spitting it out into the river's flow.

She shivered and turned her attention to the constable who held out a clipboard to her, then scribbled her name where indicated and dipped under the cordon beside her colleague. Pausing to don protective coveralls and booties, they made their way closer to where the team worked.

The man's body had been untangled from gnarly tree roots that twisted and curled between the riverbank and the water, and now lay outstretched on a black tarpaulin while a group of crime scene investigators worked with the divers and waded through the shallows, their heads bowed.

She spotted Ferguson talking to one of the uniformed officers and wandered across to them, raising her voice to be heard over the roar of the weir that cascaded from the upper reaches of the

Thames and into the pool where her colleagues worked.

'Sergeant Stanton – DC Jan West, and my colleague DC Caroline Roberts. Were you first on scene?'

The officer nodded. 'We got a call from a guest at the bed and breakfast place down the lane. He was out for a morning jog, and saw the bloke's body half out the water.'

'Any idea what happened to him?'

'He's got a head injury – a blow to the back of his skull,' said Ferguson. 'Whether that's from falling in, or an attack, it's too early to say yet. He hasn't been in the water long, but I won't be able to tell you if the head injury was the cause of death, until I do the post mortem.'

Jan wrinkled her nose. 'Kennedy's already pissed off – three deaths in less than a week. How soon can you do the PM?'

Ferguson shot her a look of disdain. 'I'll let you know. He's not the only dead body I'm dealing with this week, thanks to Gillian.'

He gave a curt nod to the police sergeant before turning his back and stomping away, his shoulders hunched.

'Grumpy bastard,' said Stanton. 'Any news on when Appleworth is back?'

'This week,' said Caroline. 'Never thought I'd be glad to see her until I had to work with him.'

'Where's the bloke who found him?' said Jan, scanning the small crowd surrounding the water's edge.

'With PC Marie Collins, back at the bed and breakfast,' said Stanton. 'He was shaken by what he saw, and we thought a hot drink would do him good. Marie will take his formal statement at the same time and I'll ask her to get that to you this afternoon.'

'Great, thanks.'

'Want to take a look while you're here?'

'Lead the way.'

Jan and Caroline followed him down the gently sloping bank towards the river where the man's body had been laid out.

As Jan drew closer, her gaze swept over the prone form.

The man appeared to be in his late twenties, with dark-brown hair and a pale complexion. His eyes gazed blankly into the middle distance, a milky haze to the irises that muted the colour and provided a shocking contrast to the bruising on his cheeks.

'What caused that?'

'Jasper's up at the weir to see if our chap hit his head on the way down,' said Stanton.

'He definitely went in there?'

'We're still processing the scene.'

'Got it.' Jan acknowledged the edge in his voice with a nod. Stanton was right – they had only been on site an hour and it would be some time yet before a full analysis was complete. 'Any other injuries apart from the head wound?'

'A few nasty marks and scratches to his face and hands. Some of the ones on his forearms are quite deep,' said Stanton, pointing them out. 'I wondered whether those might've been caused by being scratched by the tree roots along the riverbank, or by some sharp metalwork on the weir.'

'Okay.' Jan took a couple of photos on her phone to share with the rest of the team on her return, rather than wait for the formal ones to be emailed by the CSIs. 'We'll leave you to it – thanks for the update.'

'No problem. We've taken fingerprints while

Ferguson was here – hopefully they'll be put through the system this afternoon as well.'

'Thanks.'

She turned, and thrust out her arms to stop herself sliding down the bank while negotiating the upwards slope in the plastic booties, then reached the cordon and stripped off the coveralls before placing them in a nearby biohazard bin.

Caroline squinted against a fine drizzle that was beginning to form and watched while the man's body was rolled into a bag. 'Do you think he's connected to Matthew and Shaun's murders?'

'I don't know.' Jan's lip curled as she watched the brake lights from the pathologist's car flash once before it disappeared around the bend. 'Hopefully the guv can lean on Ferguson to cough up something to help us over the next couple of days. In the meantime, we'd better hope those fingerprints turn up something useful.'

CHAPTER THIRTY-NINE

Weary from a frustrating afternoon speaking to residents and dog walkers in the vicinity of Abingdon Lock, Jan followed Caroline into the incident room and sank into her chair with a sigh.

From the atmosphere around her, she suspected Kennedy would have a hard time generating some enthusiasm from the team.

A group of four uniformed officers entered the room, takeaway coffee cups in hand as they unfastened stab vests and removed hats, their conversation subdued. Many of the people they had attempted to speak to about the dead man had been out at work or elsewhere, with a long list of addresses that would have to be followed up over the course of the next twenty-four hours adding to an already substantial workload.

Jan lowered her head as the detective chief inspector for the Local Policing Area left Kennedy's office, and busied herself with sorting through the new emails that had appeared in her absence until the man disappeared into the corridor outside.

Alex wandered over, his tie askew and his shirtsleeves rolled up. 'Anything?'

'Nothing of any use. Until Ferguson can tell us when that bloke fell in the water and how long he's been there, it's hard to pinpoint a timeline for the questions we've been asking residents – those that we've been able to speak to, anyway.' She paused as Kennedy emerged from his office and waved everyone over to the whiteboard. 'Come on – maybe somebody else has had better luck than us.'

The DI didn't hang around opening the briefing.

'Where are we with the interviews in relation to Shaun Mansell's murder? Who's got an update for me?'

'Me, guv.' Alex pulled out his notebook, ran his gaze over the contents, and then raised his voice. 'We've spoken to owners of off-licences in the immediate vicinity of Shaun's flat with regard to the bottle of whisky found in the bin. All but one of them sells it, so we were slowed down by the fact we had to then obtain security camera footage from each of them and then analyse it.'

Kennedy held up his hand to stop Alex, and craned his neck to the back of the group. 'Where are we with the sketch of the person Shaun's neighbour saw?'

'It got emailed over to us five minutes ago,' said Tracy. 'I'll upload it into the database after the briefing.'

'As soon as she does, Alex, I want you to work with Marie to see if anyone on that security footage matches the sketch. Alice – what's happening with that removals company? Have you spoken to anyone there yet?'

'I did, guv.' The police constable brushed past two sergeants to reach the front of the room, and then turned to face her colleagues. 'They started their shift in Wallingford that morning, and said that the new owner of that house opposite Shaun's didn't take possession of the keys until one o'clock that afternoon. They were under pressure to finish unloading by five o'clock because their boss had agreed to a fixed term price for the job. Apart from speaking to a neighbour who wanted to know how much longer they were going to be so he could get his car out of his driveway, they didn't notice anyone else. I showed them a photo of Shaun, but neither of them can state categorically that they saw him during the day.'

'Bugger.' Kennedy poked his reading glasses further up his nose and then glared at Jan. 'And what about our other dead man?'

'No identification on him, and Ferguson wasn't prepared to venture an opinion on whether his head injury was sustained because he fell from the weir or was caused by being bashed,' said Jan. 'I asked when we could expect the post mortem to be done, but he wouldn't commit to a date – says he's overworked because Gillian isn't around—'

Kennedy's eyes narrowed. 'I'll call him in a minute to stick a rocket up his backside, the pompous arse. We need that report this week if we're going to try to ascertain if this is related to Matthew and Shaun's murders. Thank Christ

Gillian's back at work later this week. What about fingerprints?'

'Those have been taken and I'll work with uniform to get them processed,' said Caroline. 'Jan's got some photos of the guy's face as well, so I'll upload those to HOLMES2 and distribute them. That way, we can get a head start before Jasper provides an update later today after they finish at the river. I'll email them to our contacts in Wiltshire Police as well, just in case they recognise him.'

'Good work, you two.' Kennedy turned to add their updates to the increasing number of notes on the whiteboard, then glanced over his shoulder. 'You're dismissed. I want some answers and a hint of progress by tomorrow morning's briefing, got that?'

A murmur of acquiescence fluttered through the incident room before chairs were pushed back and the team dispersed to their allocated desks.

Jan wandered back to her computer, her energy ebbing as she scrolled through the emails that seemed to breed in her absence.

Half an hour later, she was contemplating taking a leaf out of her uniformed colleagues' book and sneaking out to find a decent cup of coffee when her phone vibrated.

She took one look at the name displayed on the screen and snatched it up, heading for the door. She swept her thumb across the screen before the call rang out.

'Hang on.'

Waiting until a gaggle of constables and administrative staff passed her, she leaned against the wall of the corridor and put the phone to her ear.

'Okay, make it quick before anyone else walks past, Sarge.'

'What was everyone doing down by the river this morning? I could see them from the house,' said Turpin, his voice urgent. 'Have they found something to do with Lucy's boat?'

Jan sighed. 'Not exactly. We've got another dead body. And before you ask, no, we don't know if it's related to Matthew's or Shaun's deaths yet.'

'What do we know?'

'Not a lot. We spent the morning doing the house-to-house enquiries around Abingdon Lock, but as you know it's an isolated place and a lot of people were out by the time we got the call-out – at work, or whatever. Uniform have left contact details in letterboxes where possible, but they're going to be back out there over the course of this evening if they have time and tomorrow morning trying to follow up with anyone who doesn't get in touch. Kennedy is like a caged tiger at the moment – the DCI was here when I got back, and I know the Chief Super is demanding updates on a regular basis.'

'Any idea who the dead bloke is?'

'Not yet. Caroline is working with uniform to put the fingerprints taken at the scene through the system – we might get a ping on those later today. He wasn't carrying any identification, but she's passed the details on to Wiltshire as well.'

'Have you got a photograph of him?'

She could hear the impatience in his voice, the pent-up emotions of the past week and Kennedy's insistence that he stay away from the incident room while the safe house was being organised proving too much for the detective sergeant.

'Jan?'

She sighed. 'All right. I'll message it through to you. What are you going to do?'

'This can't wait until uniform have a chance to get back to the people who live on that towpath tomorrow morning,' said Turpin. 'At least one of Lucy's neighbours spotted a man walking past the boats with Hamish on a lead. I'll head down there tonight and see what I can find out.'

CHAPTER FORTY

Mark gave a grim nod to the uniformed constable standing at his garden gate, then tugged down his woollen hat and shoved his hands in his pockets.

Hurrying from the cul-de-sac, he picked up his pace as he reached the main road and tried to batten down the worry that nibbled and frayed at his nerves.

The fresh memory of Lucy's face as he had explained the need to leave the house for a couple of hours clouded his thoughts and wove guilt around his heart, the sadness in her eyes reflecting a reluctant acceptance that he would not stop until the people who had destroyed her home and nearly killed her and his beloved daughters were brought to justice.

He had left the girls packing their bags, ready to be spirited away the next night with their mother once she arrived, their faces stoical.

It hurt him to see how well they were coping, how they simply accepted that this was what his life and theirs had become over the past few years.

No wonder Debbie had divorced him.

A restlessness had seized him throughout the day, worsened by his phone call to Jan.

He knew he should let his colleagues progress the investigation without him for a day or so while he cared for his family, but it was the nightmares that came to him in the small hours that swayed him.

This was personal, and so he would do everything he could to track down the man responsible and stop him.

The remainder of his walk passed in a blur – the bus driver who glared at him for stepping out in front of his vehicle while he was pulling away from the kerb, the woman who took one look at his face and scurried past clutching her handbag closer to her body as if to ward him off, and the two teenagers that gave him sullen stares as he stalked by – he noticed none of them as he edged closer to the path that wound its way across the meadow to the river.

Wendy Keller was nowhere to be seen when he neared the towpath, but a slightly stooped man stood on the stern, a puff of cigarette smoke lingering above him as he turned at Mark's greeting.

'Help you?'

'Detective Sergeant Mark Turpin, Thames Valley Police.' Mark held up his warrant card and tilted his face away from the smoke trail escaping from the man's nostrils as he leaned closer.

'You're Lucy's bloke?'

'Yes.'

The man held out his hand. 'David Keller. Wendy said she'd spoken to you on Saturday. Any news yet on what caused the fire?'

'Not yet, no. I was hoping you might be able to help, actually. My colleagues came past earlier but you were both out.'

'Food shop. That business with Lucy's boat has shaken us up to be honest, especially as there's a rumour it was started on purpose. Wendy wants to head down river for a while.'

'Are you going soon?'

Keller shrugged. 'In the morning, not tonight. Why?'

In response, Mark pulled out his phone and opened up the image Jan had sent him. 'Would you mind taking a look at this man to see if you recognise him? I'm sorry – it's not a pretty sight, but it's the only one I've got. He was found washed up near the weir this morning.'

'Ah, is that what all the fuss was about? I heard something about your lot being back here earlier today. Thought it was to do with the fire. Hang on – I'll get my reading glasses. Can't see a bloody thing without them.'

Keller stabbed out his cigarette in a sand-filled ceramic pot near the door and then disappeared into the cabin for a moment, returning with his wife at his heels.

'Detective Turpin? David said you had a photo to show him.'

'Is that okay? I did tell him it's of a dead man.'

He saw it then – the flash of delight in the

woman's eyes – and bit back a sigh. Speaking to potential witnesses could be a gamble at times – often the people he spoke to knew nothing, but wanted to find out more so they could tell their friends and anyone else who would listen.

Wendy's arm looped around her husband's waist as they both peered at his phone screen, then she shook her head. 'I don't know him – do you, love?'

'Never seen him before. From around here, is he?'

'We don't have that information at this time,' said Mark, shoving the phone back into his pocket. He made a point of looking at his watch, and gave an apologetic smile. 'I'm sorry – I have to get on. Will you let us know if you do happen to recall if you've seen him in the vicinity of the river in the past two weeks or so?'

'Of course,' said David.

'Thanks.'

Mark hurried away, the sound of Wendy's voice quizzing her husband about what might have been said before she appeared on the deck fading into the background as he cast his gaze across the river to the ornate slopes of the Abbey Gardens.

He would leave uniform to speak with the residents along that side of the river to conclude their house-to-house enquiries, but he wanted to find one more person before returning to his daughters.

James spotted him as he approached the narrowboat at the farthest mooring, and raised his hand in greeting when he drew closer.

'Detective Turpin. You look like you could use a drink.'

Mark stepped onto the shallow stern deck and shook the man's hand. 'I shouldn't—'

The boat owner raised a bushy eyebrow. 'You're not on duty, are you?'

'Well, no but—'

'Right then. Come on in.'

Resting his hand on the roof of the cabin for a moment, Mark let James go ahead and cast his gaze across the meadow, and then to the footpath that continued along the riverbank to the Abingdon lock.

Memories of walks with Hamish over the summer clouded his thoughts, a dull ache forming at the back of his throat as he wondered what had happened to the small dog.

It was the not knowing that hurt. The truth would be unbearable when he found out, but he needed to know. Needed to find out who was responsible.

'You coming, or what?' James barked from the depths of the narrowboat.

'Sorry.' Mark ducked under the door frame and stepped down into the galley area to find the man tipping generous measures of scotch into two glasses. 'Really, I shouldn't – I need to get back to my daughters and Lucy in a minute.'

'It's only the one. Besides, it'll be a cold walk back for you.'

Mark accepted the drink James held out, and toasted his host before taking a sip. 'Thanks.'

'Not a bother. Right, I take it you want to ask me something?'

Waiting until the man took a seat beside a small table sticking out from one side of the cabin, Mark leaned against the galley worktop and pulled out his phone. 'It's about the dead bloke who was found along by the weir this morning. I wondered if you recognised him?'

James took the phone, scowled at the image, and then leaned forward. 'I wonder…'

'What?'

'How tall was he? Do you know?'

'About five foot eight, according to the details we have so far.'

'It might've been him.'

'Where? Here?'

James handed back the phone. 'Yes. I suppose it could've been the bloke I saw with Hamish.'

'How sure are you?'

'Not one hundred per cent. But it's that Roman nose. A bit prominent, that's all.' He shrugged. 'But like I said, it was dark at the time so I only got a glimpse of him as he walked past the cabin lights.'

Mark drained the dribble of scotch at the bottom of the glass and slid it onto the worktop.

'Thanks, James. If you're right about him, the next drink's on me.'

CHAPTER FORTY-ONE

When Jan walked into the incident room the next morning, she was surprised to see Heather Bankside, the fire officer, alongside DI Kennedy at the whiteboard.

Placing her handbag under her desk, she hurried over to join them as Kennedy flipped through the pages of a bound report.

Heather gave a small smile. 'Morning, Jan.'

'Morning. Is that your final report?'

'As good as it's going to get, with what was left.'

'What's your conclusion?'

The woman grimaced. 'Mark was right. We've

confirmed that the fire was caused by an accelerant – probably petrol.'

'A petrol bomb? How?' Kennedy leafed through the report.

'Our investigators found evidence that one of the windows had been broken. It was an older boat, and Lucy confirmed the windows were only single pane, rather than double glazed. There were a few remnants of glass scattered on the inside of the hull. Some matched that of the shards remaining in the window frames, but others were of a different kind – similar to a milk bottle, or something like that. The other windows that cracked due to the heat exploded outwards, not inwards. Once we sifted through the wreckage and sorted out what we had, it was quite evident that this was an act of arson. Someone broke a window, and threw in a petrol bomb.'

'What I don't understand is how no-one saw anyone leaving Lucy's boat once the petrol bomb was thrown,' said Jan. 'Surely, whoever did that would have been in a hurry to get away – they would have stood out along that towpath because everybody knows each other.'

'It was dark by then.' Kennedy tapped a name

on the board. 'From what Mark told me this morning about Lucy's neighbours, only one of them thinks he might have seen Hamish being walked by someone prior to the fire, and none of the other boat owners saw anything – they were all inside their own cabins and came out to see what was going on when they heard Lucy's boat go up in flames.'

Heather tapped her hand against Kennedy's arm. 'Well, I'll leave that mystery to you to solve. I've got to head back – I'll drop a couple of extra copies of our report on your desk on my way out, and you should have an email in your inbox with it attached for distribution to your team.'

The DI thanked the fire officer, then turned his attention back to the whiteboard. 'It takes a special sort of arsehole to try to threaten a man's family like this.'

'Guv!'

Jan turned at the sound of Alex's voice to see the detective constable hurrying towards them.

'What is it?' said Kennedy.

'I've just had a phone call back from Wiltshire police,' he said. 'It's about the photographs we sent them of the dead guy found by the weir yesterday. They know who he is.'

'Who?' said Jan.

'Dean Evans. Plus, they've given us a list of his known associates, and all but one of them have been accounted for – Colin Hadleigh. He was the one who Mark and his bosses in Wiltshire suspected of being the leader of a county lines drugs gang they were trying to put away when he got stabbed. No-one's seen or heard anything about him for months.'

'Give me that,' said Kennedy, snatching Alex's notebook from him and running his gaze down the page. 'They've got fingerprints for our Mr Evans?'

'Only by chance,' said Alex. 'Eight years ago, he was done for drunk driving. I've had the laboratory run the fingerprints through our system to compare them with the ones we found on the whisky bottle found in the bins outside Shaun Mansell's flat, and they're a close match. I've asked the lab to let us have their report as soon as possible.'

He took his notebook from Kennedy's outstretched hand, and continued. 'Wiltshire sent through some better images as well, so I figured we could show those to Frank Tyler – see if he can confirm that's who he saw at Mansell's place.'

'Do that,' said Kennedy. 'And speak to the off-licence owners within a two-mile radius of Mansell's flat as well, show them the photos and see if it jogs their memories. Chase up the CCTV images for the roads closest to the Abbey Gardens as well – those haven't been sent yet.'

As Alex strode back to his desk, Jan turned her attention to the notes and theories that covered the whiteboard in different coloured pens.

'What do you think, guv? A team of two setting out to silence Mark and Matthew and anyone else involved in that original investigation in Swindon?'

'Maybe,' said the DI. 'And, just maybe, those two had a falling out that led to one of them ending up dead. Whatever's going on, it's linked to Mark. We need to find Colin Hadleigh before he tries to kill anyone else.'

CHAPTER FORTY-TWO

Mark twitched the living room curtain aside for the nth time, and fought down the panic that clutched at his chest.

Upstairs, he could hear Louise and Anna bickering as they packed their bags before Lucy's soothing tones calmed the noise. Footsteps sounded on the carpet above, the uneven floorboards creaking as someone moved across the room, and then he heard the tell-tale sound of Lucy's boots on the stairs.

'Everything all right?' he said over his shoulder, his eyes sweeping the entry into the cul-de-sac.

'Minor argument averted.' She wandered over to where he stood, wrapped her arms around him and rested her forehead against his shoulder. 'They're stressed out, that's all.'

'I know.' He let the curtain drop into place, turned and pulled her tighter to him. 'How are you holding up?'

She shrugged. 'Okay, I suppose. Better today. I think it's helped having so much to sort out with the boat. You?'

'Scared shitless about what Debbie's going to say when she finds out what's been going on.'

'Sarge?'

He let her go as John Newton appeared in the doorway, the constable looking younger than his years wearing jeans and a sweatshirt instead of his uniform.

'Yes?'

'Just got word your wife's about ten minutes away, Sarge. Kennedy says you need to go to the door with your daughters so if your house is being watched, it'll look like you're all planning to stay inside. We've switched them into a local taxi so everything'll look normal, rather than have her dropped off in a pool car.'

'Okay; thanks, John. Where's Kennedy at the moment?'

'On his way. He'll park a few streets away, and then use the footpath that runs along the back of your property to get here. We'll be using that route to get everyone out later tonight.'

Newton reached for his radio as it began to hiss once more, and disappeared towards the kitchen to liaise with his colleagues.

Mark could hear the voices of two more plainclothes officers as he joined them. PS Peter Cosley and another constable, Carl Ansty had taken over the kitchen table as a centre of their operations since the previous evening and were gradually eating their way through the contents of his refrigerator.

'I'd best go upstairs and get them,' said Mark. 'Will you be all right here for a moment?'

'Sure.' Lucy hugged her thick cardigan around her waist and sank into an armchair.

He left her nibbling at a thumbnail, and hurried upstairs. 'Girls, your mum's going to be here in a minute.'

Louise appeared at the door to the spare room, her face thunderous. 'Are you going to argue?'

'Probably.' He gave her a weary smile. 'I've sort of got it coming to me, haven't I?'

'Oh, Dad.' She crossed the carpet, wiping at the tears that ran down her cheeks. 'Will she let us see you again?'

Mark hugged her, stunned. He hadn't even considered the fact that Debbie might stop all his rights to see his daughters after the events of the past week, but Louise's words made his thoughts reel.

What if she did?

Could he blame her?

'I hope not,' he murmured. 'Not forever. Maybe just for a while, until we know you're all safe and we have this bastard locked away.'

'Well, I'm still going to visit.' Anna stood in the doorway, her arms folded, her face defiant.

'Thanks, love. Let's see how things pan out, shall we? I don't want to put too much pressure on your mum at the moment. She's got enough going on.'

Louise drew away at the sound of a car pulling up outside. 'Is that her?'

'I'd imagine so. All packed?' Mark forced cheer into his voice, and walked into the bedroom.

Both of the girls' suitcases were on the bed, and he picked up each before heading towards the stairs. 'Come on. We need you both at the door to greet her.'

The girls followed him down the stairs, and he placed the suitcases next to the base of the newel post before embracing each of them in turn.

'Dry your eyes, come on. It'll be okay.'

A figure appeared on the other side of the frosted glass panel at the top of the door, and he swung it open to find Debbie standing beside a plainclothes officer who averted her eyes as his ex-wife strode into the house.

She glared at him, then pulled her daughters into a fierce hug.

'If that's all, Sarge, I'll – erm – I'll pay the taxi driver and head off,' said PC Collins, embarrassment colouring her cheeks.

'Thanks, Marie.' Mark took the suitcase she held out and closed the door, aware that the voices in the kitchen had grown silent.

There was no noise from the living room either, as if Lucy was holding her breath.

Eventually, Debbie released their daughters and spun on her heel to face him.

'Mark? What the bloody hell has been going on?'

CHAPTER FORTY-THREE

A faint trace of cigarette smoke followed Peter Cosley in from the back garden as he closed the kitchen door.

'We're ready,' he said. 'Coast is clear.'

John Newton hovered at the kitchen table, his eyes troubled. 'They need to go now, Sarge. No hanging around.'

'I'll go and get them.'

He left his colleagues in the kitchen, both John Newton and the other constable still visibly embarrassed by the argument he and Debbie had had earlier, despite their retreating upstairs and closing the door to the spare room he used as an office.

She had calmed down eventually, but it would be a long time before he would be forgiven.

Maybe never.

As he entered the living room, a frosty silence met his arrival, and Lucy looked up from one of his motorbike magazines she was feigning interest in as he cleared his throat.

'Debbie? They're here to take everyone to the safe house.'

His ex-wife glared up from the board game she was playing with Anna and Louise, then pursed her lips. 'You heard your father, girls. Get your coats.'

Mark helped Anna into her fake-fur-lined anorak and hugged her before turning to Louise. 'Keep an eye on your mum and sister for me, all right?'

Her bottom lip quivered, but she nodded, then followed Anna out to the kitchen.

'Lucy? You too.'

'What?' She looked up from the magazine and frowned. 'I thought I was staying here.'

'No, you're going with them.' He glanced at

Debbie. 'If that's too awkward, then let Kennedy know and he'll make alternative arrangements tomorrow, but you're not staying here.'

She sighed, tossed the magazine to one side, and followed him and Debbie into the hallway.

'Hang on.' His ex-wife held up a hand to stop him. 'If you're right about all of this, then aren't you in danger as well? Why aren't you coming with us?'

'Because we're going to lure whoever's doing this here,' said Mark. 'We're going to end this, one way or the other.'

'Can't they do that without you?'

'Not really. It needs to look like I'm here, after all.'

They broke off as the kitchen door opened and Jan walked in, followed by Ewan Kennedy.

'Everybody ready?' she said.

'Yes.' Mark gestured to Debbie and Lucy to join the girls. 'As ready as we will be.'

'Wait – Mark?' His ex-wife placed her hand on his arm. 'What if something happens to you?'

'It won't. Not with this lot here with me. It'll be fine, trust me.'

She didn't respond, but instead watched as

Newton handed the suitcases to a sergeant who hovered at the door.

'Let's go,' said Kennedy, his voice gruff. He made way for Anna, then beckoned to Louise and Debbie. 'Come on.'

'I'll see you soon.' Lucy swung her tote bag over her shoulder and gave him a kiss on the cheek. 'Behave yourself, all right?'

'Promise. Like I said, it'll be fine.'

She followed the others and he moved to the window, peering into the darkened garden beyond.

'Do you think they believe you?' said Jan, raising her hand in farewell as the kitchen door swung shut.

Mark waved to his daughters as they glanced back at him through the window, the moonlight catching their hair before they disappeared after Kennedy and PC Ansty through the back gate. Despite the smile plastered to his face as Debbie and Lucy followed them, he gritted his teeth.

'Not a chance in hell.'

Jan snorted, then pulled him away. 'Come on, put the kettle on. Scott's got a couple of his mates around tonight to watch a premiership game on the telly so I don't have to go just yet. What about you lot? Who's staying tonight?'

'Me and John will be here until midnight,' said Cosley. 'Wilcox is sorting out a couple of constables to take over from then through to six o'clock tomorrow morning. Kennedy says that we'll watch your movements between here and the station in the morning from a distance. Just act normal.'

'Is that the plan for the rest of the week?' said Mark.

'Pretty much.' Cosley grinned. 'If you want to get rid of us, better hope we catch this bastard soon.'

'Noted.'

They jumped at a knock on the kitchen door.

'Shit, what now?' Mark wrenched it open, then took a step back in surprise. 'Lucy?'

'There's no way I'm sharing a house with your ex-wife, the mood she's in,' she said, stomping over the threshold. 'Hello again, everyone.'

'What did Kennedy say?' Mark closed the door, confused. 'You could be in danger if you stay here, you know that.'

'He said something about my being as stubborn as you.' She grinned, and held up the tote bag. Something inside clinked. 'So, do you want some of this wine I brought with me earlier, or what?'

'I think you're probably the bravest woman I know,' he said, pulling her into his arms. 'Either that, or the craziest.'

CHAPTER FORTY-FOUR

Bleary-eyed after a sleepless night worrying about his family and unable to rest due to the knowledge two colleagues were staying in his living room in the event of immediate danger, Mark failed to suppress an enormous yawn as he rang the intercom for Oxford's mortuary.

'Of all the days...' he muttered before turning to his colleague.

'Look on the bright side,' said Jan. 'She probably vented most of her anger chatting to Debbie last night.'

'God, I hope so.' Mark groaned, and loosened

the tie at his neck, rolling it up and shoving it in his pocket.

'Was Lucy all right this morning?'

'Tired. I left her on the phone to the insurers again. And some banks, to see if she can get a loan. You know what insurers' interpretation of the market value of a car is like? It turns out boats are even worse.'

'She's not on her own there?'

'No – Kennedy switched the watch shift at six o'clock this morning.' He turned at the sound of a faint buzzing, the lock mechanism clicking free, and placed his hand on the door handle. 'Here we go, then.'

Gillian Appleworth, the Home Office pathologist who also happened to be his ex-sister-in-law, looked up from the reception desk where she'd been speaking to her assistant, and glared at him.

'You've got some bloody explaining to do,' she said, her tone as frosty as the chill air that emanated from the open door into the morgue.

'Morning, Gillian.' He could hear the forced cheer in his voice, knowing he was baiting her as he signed in and took a set of protective coveralls from Clive, but unable to resist.

If he was going to get a reprimand, he might as well get it over with.

He sidled out of the way to let Jan reach the visitors' log book and locked eyes with the pathologist. 'Is she all right?'

Gillian pursed her lips. 'Scared. Angry.'

'And you?'

'Pissed off.' Her shoulders relaxed a little. 'Is it true? Is this all about what happened in Swindon?'

'We think so. I'm the only plausible connection to the murders so far, especially the first one – Matthew.'

'Were you warned? Did you refuse to back off or something like that?' Her tone was urgent now, and he recognised the note of panic.

'No, no warnings.' He lowered his gaze to his feet as Jan finished speaking with Clive and joined them. 'I'm going to stop him, Gillian. He went too far this time. I know I'm in the firing line in this job – I sort of expect to be sometimes – but the minute someone tries to kill my family…'

He looked up when she sighed, and watched while she buttoned up her protective gown.

'So the two murders last week, and possibly this man's death, are all down to the same person?' she said.

'We think so, yes.'

'You need to stop him, Mark. Before he stops you.'

'Then help me find who's responsible. Help us put him away – for good.'

'Oh, Mark.' Her grey eyes closed for a moment before she shook her head and beckoned to him. 'Come on. Let's get this over with.'

He exhaled, then let Jan go ahead as he brought up the rear of the sad procession towards the examination room.

Gillian spent the first five minutes giving Clive instructions about how she was going to proceed with the post mortem, an unusual procedure for the otherwise synchronised team of two, and she shot Mark a glare as Clive began sorting through various implements that would be needed.

'That idiot Ferguson left this place in such a state of chaos, it's going to take us a week to find everything,' she said, waving a nasty-looking saw. 'Bear with us, we'll begin in a minute.'

Mark took a step backwards as the pathologist swept past, unwilling to get in her way and further worsen her mood.

'If it's any consolation, we missed you too.'

She glared at him, but he caught the twitch at the side of her mouth before she looked away and focused her attention on the prone body of Dean Evans, placing her hand on the microphone switch above the table to activate it.

Mark tuned out as the examination progressed, averting his eyes as the large saw whirred to life and cut through the man's sternum.

Gillian provided a clear commentary as she worked, passing various organs and samples to Clive, who expertly tipped them into weighing scales before preparing them for laboratory analysis.

Finally, it was over.

He and Jan moved a little closer as Clive began to stitch the man back together, and Mark adjusted his mask to try to offset the stench emanating from the man's abdomen.

'Do you have an opinion about time of death?' said Jan.

'I'd say he's been out there two days at most,' said Gillian, pulling her mask away. 'The damage to his eyes has likely been caused by wildlife along that stretch of the river – foxes, rats, that sort of thing.'

'He wasn't spotted until Monday morning, though.' Jan frowned. 'If you're saying he went in the water about two days ago, then that's around Friday night or Saturday morning.'

'The eddies in that part of the Thames are strong, especially the currents at the foot of the weir where they meet the lock,' said Mark. 'Plus, he was wearing dark-coloured clothing. His body might've been caught in the churn below the weir for a while before he broke loose and got washed up on the shoreline.'

'Or he was swept out straight away and got stuck in the tree branches,' said Jan. 'I've got a contact at the Environment Agency – I'll give her a call later today to see if either theory is possible.'

'So, what do you think, Gill? Accident or murder?' said Mark, eager to bring the post mortem to a close and escape the confines of the mortuary.

The pathologist ran her gaze down the length of the man's body. 'I'm fairly confident the wound to the back of his head wasn't caused by his falling over the weir. The safety barriers above the weir are only waist height for someone like Dean, and it wouldn't have taken much to pitch him over the side. So, I'd say he had help, yes.'

'What about the cuts and bruising to his hands and arms?' said Jan. 'I wondered whether those might have been caused by metalwork on the weir, or perhaps the tree branches along the side of the riverbank. Or are they defensive wounds?'

Gillian gently picked up one of the dead man's hands between her own and turned it to better see the marks under the overhead lighting, and gestured to them to move closer.

'Not metal or wood, but most likely made by an animal. Look, you can see the bite marks here – some of them are quite deep. The scratches up around his wrist and forearms are similar to claws as well. He's had a struggle with a dog at some point before his death – they're definitely not post mortem.'

'Maybe he was the one who Lucy's neighbour saw with Hamish that night,' said Jan. 'And maybe Hamish put up a fight if Evans was trying to… trying to ki—'

She didn't finish the sentence and lowered her gaze.

'Good.' Mark ran his eyes over the deep cuts. 'With any luck, it fucking hurt.'

CHAPTER FORTY-FIVE

Jan finished her call and spun her chair around to face Turpin.

The detective sergeant had his phone to his ear, but caught her eye and nodded.

While she waited, she looked around the incident room and tried to take in the sheer amount of information that the team were trying their best to process.

Every desk was taken by the time the clock on the wall showed half past four in the afternoon as uniformed officers, detectives and administrative staff worked to update the database, chased up leads and loose ends, and scurried back and forth between their computers and the printers.

All so that DI Kennedy could be presented with the most detailed briefing materials possible at the end of the day.

Anything that could demonstrate some sort of progress.

Her colleagues' despondency was tangible.

'Jan – sorry about that. What've you got?'

Turpin's voice jolted her from her reverie, and she blinked to refocus.

'Right, yes.' She leaned forward and pointed at her computer screen as he moved around their desks to join her. 'I pulled up this satellite image of Abingdon Lock, and the weir alongside it. Jenny Foster from the Environment Agency phoned back five minutes ago. She confirms that if someone fell into the water below the weir's sluice gates, then it's entirely possible that the eddies and currents along that stretch of water would tug that body along the bank of the river to the right here, and it may well end up caught up along the bank where Dean Evans' body was found on Monday morning.'

'Can you zoom in so I can take a closer look?'

'I can, but people have uploaded photos of the weir over the years because it forms part of the Thames Path, and they provide an even better angle. Look.'

Jan waited while Turpin flicked through the various images. He paused when he reached one showing a group of people alongside the safety fencing.

'Gillian was right. That barrier isn't as high as I recall. It'd be less than waist high on me, only a bit more than she reckoned it would be for Dean Evans.'

'That's not all, Sarge.' Jan turned from the screen to face him. 'I went down there again this afternoon, and part of the fencing is dented – sort of caved in a bit, as if something heavy leaned against it. I did ask Jasper to send someone out to see if they could find any evidence, but there have been too many walkers along there since Monday. Any fingerprints or fibres that might've been traced back to Dean's clothing are gone.'

'Shit.' Turpin's shoulders slumped as his phone rang once more. 'Thanks for following it up, anyway.'

'Got him.'

Jan raised her head and looked over to where Alex sat at his desk, a look of triumph on his features as he waved her over.

Turpin held up his hand in a waiting gesture, and murmured into his desk phone, his words hurried.

'Who?' She pushed back her chair, ignoring the clatter it made as it crashed against a filing cabinet, and crossed the room.

'Dean Evans. Look.' Alex waited until Turpin finished his call and joined them, then pointed at the screen. 'I was going through the CCTV footage at Didcot Parkway again – last time we viewed it, we were concentrating on Matthew, but this is definitely Evans. Watch.'

He hit the play button, and tapped his finger on the screen as a hooded man left a Reading-bound train. 'You'll see his face in a minute.'

The figure on the video kept his head bowed, shoved his hands in the pockets of his hoodie and jogged down the stairs to the subway beneath the platforms. Alex reached out for his mouse, changed the view to a second camera on the outside of the station concourse, and paused the recording as the man exited the ticket office and raised his gaze to the list of times displayed on an electronic board beside the bus stop.

'It's definitely him,' said Turpin. 'Well spotted. What time was this?'

Alex double-checked his notes against the list of footage that had been provided to them. 'Half two on Monday afternoon.'

'Only hours before Matthew was killed,' said Jan, disgusted. 'He was sent here to murder him, wasn't he? And then he killed Shaun Mansell as well.'

'Either that, or he came here to make sure Shaun killed Matthew, and then murdered him to keep him quiet. I showed the photos we got from Wiltshire to Frank Tyler this morning – Shaun's neighbour – and he said he reckoned Dean Evans was the bloke he saw leaving Shaun's flat.'

'But then who killed Evans?' said Alex. 'I've been working through the footage, and there's no sign of Colin Hadleigh. If he's responsible for Evans' death, then you'd expect him to follow.'

'The Wiltshire lot said that he hasn't been seen in months,' said Jan.

'He doesn't need to be seen. A lot of his contacts might be accounted for, but he'll have a network of people he can turn to in an emergency – people who he can threaten if they don't help him. Hang on – I've had a thought.' Turpin raised his voice. 'Caroline – can you find out whether we've had any reports of licence plates being stolen in the days leading up to our three murders?'

'Sure – give me a moment.'

Jan frowned. 'Sarge?'

He turned back to her. 'That was an old colleague from Wiltshire I was speaking to on the phone. One of Hadleigh's associates' cars was pinged by the system on the outskirts of Swindon on Friday night before it turned onto the A420.'

'That's heading towards Oxford, isn't it?'

'Exactly. The thing is, the car stopped before the next camera, and hasn't been since.'

'Did he switch the plates?'

'That's what Wiltshire think.'

'Here you go, Sarge.' Caroline waved them over, then ran her gaze down a report on her screen. 'Someone phoned the non-emergency number on Monday night to say his plates were stolen off his car while he was with his kids in a fast food place on the outskirts of Shrivenham.'

'All right,' said Turpin. 'That's the licence plate you need to run through ANPR from Shrivenham onwards.'

'Got you.'

'Once you've got confirmation he's here in Abingdon, get Tom to sort you out with a couple of people from uniform to help you and Alex go through the CCTV again for the period from Matthew's murder through to Monday morning when Dean Evans' body was found in the river.'

He tapped the photograph of Colin Hadleigh in the open file on the detective constable's desk. 'He's here, and I want to know how the hell he got near Lucy's boat without anyone seeing him.'

CHAPTER FORTY-SIX

Mark rubbed his hands down his face and bit back a yawn.

A stale atmosphere filled the incident room – the sky beyond the windows had been dark for the past hour, and the mutterings of an exhausted investigative team underpinned the sound of phones ringing.

Car headlights reflected off the sills as the last of the town's commuters passed the building on their way out of the industrial estate and on towards the main road that would take them home.

And yet, no-one moved from their desks, faces

caught in the glow from computer screens as they worked.

During any investigation, the incident room would be filled with the noise expected from a group of people working long hours within close proximity of each other, but at this late hour, exhaustion had crept in, and the only voices that carried across to where he sat were muted, contemplative.

Kennedy had kept the afternoon briefing short, and Mark guessed that he had wanted the team back to work as soon as possible, given the lack of progress to date.

And the frustration that came with it.

'Sarge? You might want to come over and take a look at this,' said Caroline, hovering next to the filing cabinets beside Jan's desk, her notebook in her hand.

Mark straightened, letting out an ill-disguised groan as his back protested after too long hunched over a computer keyboard. He rolled his shoulders while he followed Caroline across to where she and Alex had been going through the CCTV footage once more.

The detective constable indicated a spare chair beside hers, then pointed at the screen.

'We've been trying to put together a timeframe of Dean's movements since he turned up at Didcot Parkway last week,' she explained. 'We know we've got him on camera in the vicinity of Shaun Mansell's flat, but after that, nothing – until Thursday night. Here.'

Mark peered at the grainy video recording on the screen.

In it, a figure wearing a woollen hat tugged low over his brow walked across a road, one hand shoved in his coat pocket while the other carried a large bag similar in shape to that of a sports holdall.

'Where is this?'

'Stert Street, just before it reaches the town square,' said Alex, rolling his chair over to join them. 'He crosses the road here, and then heads past the Guildhall. CCTV picks him up on Abbey Close, heading towards the river before we lose him.'

'What's in the bag, I wonder?' said Mark. 'We haven't found that, have we?'

'Not yet, Sarge.' Caroline jerked her thumb towards Alex. 'He's got a theory about it, though.'

Her colleague's cheeks flushed. 'It's just an idea.'

'Well, let's have it,' said Mark, leaning back in his chair.

'I was thinking about the size of the bag he's carrying, Sarge. And the shape. It's a bit boxy-looking, isn't it? I mean, if Hadleigh had sent him here to silence Matthew and Shaun Mansell then I wouldn't expect him to be carrying something that size. He'd be travelling light, wouldn't he? Maybe a backpack or something at most.'

Mark looked at the frozen image on the screen once more, and frowned. 'It looks on the heavy side, too. Bulky.'

'Exactly.' Alex's voice grew louder as he warmed to his subject. 'So, what I was thinking… The thing is, me and my girlfriend spent a lot of time in the summer mucking about on the river when it was hot, and we were thinking of buying ourselves a kayak for next year. It'd be cheaper than hiring them all the time like we did this year—'

'Right…' Mark cocked an eyebrow at

Caroline, wondering where Alex was headed with his explanation but she smiled and gestured for him to wait and listen.

'Anyway, we're renting a one-bedroom flat in the middle of town. No room for a kayak,' said Alex. 'We'd kind of given up on the idea, until Becky finds out you can buy inflatable kayaks.'

'Inflatable kayaks?'

'Yeah. You just pump it up at the water's edge when you want to use it, then deflate it to put it back in storage. It only weighs about fifteen kilograms, too.' Alex leaned forward and tapped the screen. 'The thing is, Sarge, the bag it comes in looks a lot like this.'

'If that's a kayak, where's the paddle?' said Jan.

'Probably in the bag,' said Alex. 'If it's like the one we were looking at, the paddle unscrews so you can either use one end each if there are two of you in the kayak, or put it together for a single user. It makes it easy to transport it, too.'

Mark looked at the image of Dean Evans once more, and then back to Alex. He blinked. 'Bloody hell, McClellan. I think you might be onto something.'

'Dean brings the kayak to Hadleigh on the Friday night,' said Caroline, 'and helps him inflate it somewhere near the water's edge, out of sight, and then walks around to the opposite side of the river, entices Hamish away from Lucy's boat—'

'—and Hadleigh paddles across once he knows Hamish won't raise the alarm, breaks a window and tosses the petrol bomb inside,' said Mark. 'He assumes Lucy and the girls were on board because the curtains were pulled and they left some lights on before going to the shops. He paddles away from the boat before the flames take hold and heads back upstream where Dean can help him deflate the kayak.'

'At which point,' said Jan, wandering over with Kennedy in tow, 'perhaps Hadleigh kills Dean and pitches his body into the river – again, to cover his tracks – before walking away, carrying this bag.'

'Have you got Hadleigh on camera with the bag?' said the detective inspector, his arms crossed as he glared at the screen.

Alex shook his head. 'No – we haven't seen him on camera at all, but I wondered if maybe he simply threw the bag in a hedge or over someone's back fence. I mean, he didn't need it anymore, did he?'

'Check downstairs in case anyone's handed it in,' said Kennedy. 'If not, then I'll organise a team in the morning to search the footpaths and roads leading away from the river. And good work, Alex.'

'Thanks, guv.'

'While I've got you all here, we've had some success in locating Hadleigh's car,' the detective inspector continued. He handed out photographs of an industrial estate. 'This is outside Challow. ANPR picked up the vehicle on the main road there on Monday night. Uniform have just wrapped up speaking with the owners of the businesses in the units there, and one of them runs a garage. Only small, mind, for vehicle testing and the like, but he confirms that a man matching Hadleigh's description turned up and said he planned to sell his car and wanted a quick once-over. He got a taxi from the place after handing over the keys.'

'Any idea where he went?'

'No,' said Kennedy, 'and the car's still there. It's being monitored in case it goes on the move again, and the owner of the business will let us know if Hadleigh returns.'

'So, we just arrest him when he comes back. Easy,' said Caroline.

'If we arrest him now, we haven't got enough to charge him with,' said Kennedy. 'He'll simply blame Dean Evans for the death of Shaun Mansell and Matthew, as well as the arson attack. We've got no evidence to suggest he was the one responsible for destroying Lucy's boat – the CCTV footage only shows Dean carrying that bag, after all.'

'He's not going to stop until he gets to me, guv,' said Mark, hearing the tiredness in his voice. 'We have to do something.'

'What do you want to do, guv?' said Jan.

Kennedy twirled the arm of his reading glasses between his fingers for a moment, then looked from her to Mark and the other detectives.

'Leave the car where it is. When it moves, we follow. With any luck, he'll head to Mark's house and we'll arrest him before he takes this any further. Get home and get some rest, all of you. We're not there yet with this one, and I have a feeling we're in for some long days.'

CHAPTER FORTY-SEVEN

Jan emitted an unladylike snort as she struggled to wake up, the shrill ring of her mobile phone wresting her from a deep sleep.

Scott switched on his bedside light, his gaze confused as he turned to face her.

'Sorry, love,' she murmured, and swiped the screen before throwing back the bedcovers. 'Guv?'

'Hadleigh is on the move. The ANPR pinged his car with the stolen licence plates leaving the industrial estate near Challow five minutes ago, and he's heading towards Grove. We have to assume he's coming for Mark. There are two patrol cars on their way to intercept him. I want you and Caroline there for the arrest because I want him brought in and interviewed straight away.'

Jan blinked back sleep, shifted her phone to her right hand and perched on the end of the mattress to pull on her trousers.

'Where's the team now?'

'They just left Didcot – they're planning to head out via Steventon and the Hanney Road – based on the fact Hadleigh is probably going to use the A338 to get to Abingdon rather than risk the dual carriageway.'

'Okay. On my way.'

'I'll let them know. Expect a phone call with an update from us soon.'

'What time is it?' Shaun yawned, pulling the blanket up over his shoulders.

'Half past three. Smoke me a kipper…'

'I doubt very much Kennedy will let you come back here for breakfast.'

Jan smiled, finished dressing and then dashed around to his side of the bed and kissed him. 'See you later.'

'Love you.'

She ran down the stairs two at a time, snatched her coat off the newel post and swung her bag over her shoulder before heading out of the front door.

The car started first time, and she floored the accelerator after clipping her phone into the dashboard mount, calling out Caroline's name as she exited the housing estate.

'Jan? You heard from Kennedy as well?' The other detective constable sounded breathless.

'About three minutes ago. I'm going to head towards Marcham – you?'

'Same. I'll probably end up behind you so I'll flash my headlights when I see you.'

'Okay.'

'Is Mark on his way?'

'I doubt it – Kennedy's probably left him sleeping.'

'Lucky bastard.'

'We'll remind him, don't worry.' Jan wound down the window a crack to alleviate the remnants of sleepiness. 'Anyway, if all this is meant to draw out Hadleigh and have him head towards Mark, it'd look a bit daft if he's not actually at home.'

'True.'

Caroline ended the call, and Jan tightened her grip on the steering wheel as she negotiated the twisting road towards the A338.

She hoped she made it in time.

She wanted to be there when Hadleigh's car was pulled over by her colleagues, and see the look on his face when he realised his efforts to murder Turpin and his family had been in vain.

And she wanted retribution for the young teenager and the men he had killed in his ruthless attempts to do so.

Lights in the distance caught her attention, and she realised she was approaching the petrol station at the junction with the main road. Her gaze flickered to the clock on the dashboard – four o'clock, and the place would be opening soon, ready to welcome the first of its early morning customers.

Gritting her teeth, cognisant that traffic would grow steadily heavier as dawn broke, she hoped they would be able to stop Hadleigh without causing injury to anyone else.

Her phone rang in its cradle, and she thumbed the button on the steering wheel to answer.

'West.'

'It's Kennedy. Hadleigh turned onto the Garford Road.'

'What?' Jan heard the confusion in her voice. 'Why? That's going in the opposite direction to Mark's house.'

'Both of our patrol cars are well back at the moment, so he wouldn't have spotted them. He could be taking a convoluted route to be on the safe side. Take the Kingston Bagpuize road and circle back on him, all right? I'll tell uniform to close the gap and between you, you should be able to bring him to a standstill before he reaches Southmoor.'

'Guv.'

She disconnected the call, then glanced in the rear-view mirror as a vehicle's headlights appeared behind and flickered twice.

Caroline had caught up with her.

Jan tapped the brakes, checked for oncoming traffic, then zipped across the junction and accelerated once more.

Her heart began to race while the training she had received years ago about vehicle pursuits flashed in her memory. Despite what people saw on television, stopping a suspect in a moving car was dangerous and neither she nor her colleagues wanted their morning to start with a tragedy.

The phone rang once more.

'He's heading your way. About a mile to go.' Kennedy's voice sounded distorted, with background noise suggesting he was pacing the floor of Force Control as they monitored the progress of the killer's vehicle on ANPR and passed his orders to the two patrol cars. 'Pull up on the next straight stretch of road you come to, use your vehicles to block his way, and get yourselves clear in case he doesn't stop.'

'Got that, guv.'

Flashing her brakes to warn her colleague, she held her breath as the car swept around the next bend. Sure enough, the road stretched ahead of her; a narrow part of the lane that left oncoming traffic nowhere to pass.

She wrenched the wheel to her left, applied the handbrake and stepped out as Caroline swept her car to the right, creating a herringbone-shaped blockade.

'Move!' Jan called, and led the way back to the bend in the road they'd just passed.

Hearing sirens in the distance, she broke into a run, reaching the safety of a farm entrance moments before the roar of an engine reached her.

'Here they come,' said Caroline, craning her neck to see beyond the parked cars.

'Glad I'm using a pool car this week,' Jan muttered. 'You?'

'It's my brother's.' Her colleague shrugged. 'Doesn't matter. It's a heap of shit anyway. He's been meaning to scrap it all year.'

Jan laughed, despite the seriousness of the situation.

Headlights pierced the pre-dawn gloom as the first vehicle rounded the curve at the far end and bore down towards the parked cars.

'Hasn't he seen them?'

She ignored her colleague's words, and instead watched Hadleigh's car.

It wasn't slowing down.

A split second later, the two patrol cars came into view, keeping a safe distance between them and the car they pursued. It would do no good if they rear-ended the vehicle after it crashed – it would only result in casualties.

Jan bit her lip as Hadleigh continued towards them.

'He's going to run out of road in a minute,' said Caroline, a note of urgency creeping into her voice.

Maybe they were wrong.

Maybe he wasn't going to stop…

'Move back,' said Jan, and pulled her colleague further into the farm entrance until they were behind a concrete pillar.

A screeching of tyres on tarmac carried along the road, and then Jan heard the unmistakable crunch and scrape of plastic trim as it met undergrowth.

The sirens stopped, and she peered around the pillar.

Hadleigh had ploughed into the hedgerow a few paces short of her car, and the two patrol cars had ground to a halt behind it.

Their killer had nowhere to go.

'Don't let him run!' she yelled, doing exactly that to reach the four uniformed officers who had launched themselves from the pursuit vehicles.

She and Caroline reached Hadleigh's car at the

same time as a lean police sergeant who looked none the worse for the sprint he had undertaken.

'Shall I?' he said, his hand on the door handle.

'Go for it,' said Jan, moving behind him and ready to read Hadleigh his rights.

As the sergeant wrenched the door open, Caroline's shocked gasp of breath mirrored her own thoughts.

A lanky youth in his early twenties sat behind the wheel, his hands raised and his eyes wide open as the torchlight swung into his face.

Bruises covered his eye socket and jawline while blood trickled from his bottom lip.

'Who the hell are you?' said Jan.

'Gary Livens. I'm sorry. He told me I had to. He said he knew where my girlfriend lived and if I didn't do as he told me, he'd kill her.'

A fat tear rolled over the man's bruised cheek.

'Shit.'

Jan walked a few paces away, pulled out her mobile phone and hit speed dial.

'Guv? Hadleigh wasn't driving the car. He's not here.'

CHAPTER FORTY-EIGHT

Mark rolled over, kicked the sheet off his feet and draped an arm across Lucy's waist.

He had at least managed to get some rest, even though his sleep had been intermittent. Despite the presence of two constables in his house, he couldn't shake the responsibility he felt for Lucy and his family.

A blackbird whistled a shrill rebuke outside. Moments later a robin joined in and he wondered if the neighbour's cat was on the prowl, making the most of the quiet before the commuting hours.

He ran his hand over gritty eyes, resisting the urge to put the light on.

Dawn was yet to break through a gap at the top of the bedroom curtains and he didn't want to move until he had to.

He savoured the sound of Lucy's soft breathing beside him, the motion of her body as she slept.

He wished everything could be how it was before.

That Lucy still had her home.

That Hamish was still alive.

That two men and a boy hadn't been murdered because one person wanted to keep control of his drugs business and flood the local area with a deadly concoction of benzodiazepines that would maim and kill even more people.

'I can hear you thinking.'

He raised his arm as Lucy rolled over to face him wearing a wry smile.

'Sorry – didn't mean to wake you.'

'You didn't. What time is it?'

He flicked his wrist and peered at the luminous dial of his watch. 'Half past four.'

'Are you going into work today?'

'Probably. I wouldn't mind finding out what

progress they've had. It's not the same hearing it over the phone.'

A loud snoring permeated the floorboards, and she giggled. 'Someone's sleeping well, at least.'

Downstairs, the toilet flushed, and Mark listened as footsteps padded down the hallway before the kitchen door was closed.

'They must be splitting the shift. Makes sense. Sitting around like that can be tiring.'

He pulled her closer, kissed the bundle of curls that framed her face and inhaled the sweet scent of her shampoo.

Her body moved against his, and he bit back a groan.

'What time do you have to go in?' she whispered.

'Not yet.'

A gentle whirring noise emanated through the window, pausing outside. Moments later, the clink of glass filtered up from the front doorstep.

'At least there'll be enough milk now when we get up,' murmured Lucy. 'I thought they were going to finish the last of it overnight.'

She snuggled under his arm and rested her cheek against his chest.

Mark lifted his head off the pillow and frowned. 'But I don't have it delivered.'

A crash from downstairs and a startled yelp from the room below sent him diving for his jeans draped over a chair beside the bed, split seconds before the stink of petrol and a terrifying *whump* roared from the direction of the living room door.

He heard Newton cry out, and then Cosley barged from the kitchen at full speed, yelling at the top of his voice.

'Fire! Fire!'

'Get dressed – now.' Mark pulled on his jeans and shoes and then helped Lucy, making sure she was heading for the stairs before he tugged a sweatshirt over his head.

He stopped on the landing, opened a cupboard and pulled blankets from it, then ran.

When he reached the bottom of the stairs, Cosley was helping Newton from the living room, the constable retching from the fumes and smoke.

'Shut the door.' Mark dropped to the floor, rolled up the blankets and shoved the material against the gap. 'Everyone all right?'

'Yes, Sarge,' the constable croaked. 'Luckily I'd just woken up when he smashed the window.'

Mark turned to see Lucy reaching for the front door handle.

'Back door, back door!' he shouted to her. 'Don't go out there – he could be waiting for us.'

She paled at his words, then nodded and sprinted towards the kitchen.

'Don't hang around – follow her,' he said to the two constables. 'Make sure it's safe, then get her out. I'll be right behind you.'

Mark chewed his lip, then dashed upstairs to the small room he used as an office.

He could hear the flames taking hold in the living room, hear the crackle and pop as his belongings fuelled the fire. Snatching up the framed sketch Lucy had given him when he moved in and a favourite photograph of his two daughters, he moved to the wardrobe and pulled out two thick coats for himself and Lucy before racing back down the stairs and out of the kitchen door.

Sirens carried on the wind as he joined Cosley at the back gate, the sergeant lowering his radio.

'Fire crews are on their way, and Kennedy's sending over a car to pick you up.'

Mark handed one of the coats to Lucy and

shrugged the other one over his shoulders before passing the two picture frames to her. Kissing her briefly, he opened the gate.

'I'm going around the front.'

'I'll come with you, Sarge,' said Cosley. 'The guv will kill me if anything happens to one of you.'

Leaving his colleague with Lucy, he fell into step behind Mark, who ran along the weed-strewn gravel path and around the corner. The path narrowed before reaching the cul-de-sac and he slid to a halt on the uneven surface.

Peering over the hedge that separated his rental property from the path, he could see no-one.

Hadleigh had gone.

CHAPTER FORTY-NINE

Jan tipped the dregs of tea into the sink, rinsed the mug and stood it on the draining rack, glancing over her shoulder at footsteps on the tiled floor.

'Sorry if we woke you, Debbie.'

Turpin's ex-wife shook her head and yawned. 'Don't worry about it. I couldn't sleep anyway. What's going on?'

She looked at the tired faces of the gathered police officers who sat around a pine table that took up most of the kitchen.

Kennedy had ordered Jan and Caroline to the safe house to brief Alex and the team there about the outcome of the early morning pursuit and to provide additional protection for the family while he contacted Turpin.

Situated on the outskirts of Abingdon, the large empty farmhouse had been selected due to its relative remoteness – the nearest neighbouring property was quarter of a mile away, and a flat landscape gave the protection team a clear view of any approaching vehicles or people.

'We thought we had Hadleigh earlier,' said Jan, unwilling to lie or soften the truth. Debbie's sole focus was on protecting her daughters, and Jan knew that if their roles were reversed, she would expect the same amount of respect. 'Unfortunately, he'd used someone else to drive his car.'

'A decoy, you mean?' Debbie zipped up the neck of her chunky sweatshirt and moved across the kitchen to the kettle, flipping it on. 'So, where is he?'

'We assumed he'd be heading towards Abingdon, which was why we were trying to intercept him. Now DI Kennedy is trying to contact Mark to warn him and the team at his house.'

'No luck yet.' Alex scowled at the AirWave

radio that spat out static from its position in the middle of the table. 'If you're having one, Debbie, I'll join you.'

Turpin's ex-wife appeared not to have heard the young detective constable, and wandered closer to where Jan leaned against the sink.

'Have you tried to phone him?'

'No. Sometimes it's better to leave one person trying to make contact – otherwise we all end up phoning and then we can't get through.' She reached out and placed her hand on the woman's arm. 'Don't worry. As soon as we know anything, either Alex or I will let you know.'

Debbie shook her head, her eyes downcast. 'I wish Lucy hadn't gone back to the house. I like her, really I do, and I didn't mean to upset her yesterday. I was just so… I was worried about Anna and Louise.'

'Of course you were. So would I be, if I were in your position.'

'You've got twin boys, haven't you?'

'Yes, and I'd be going up the wall if I thought they were in danger.'

Peering through the window as the morning

sun crested a copse of trees at the end of the large garden, Debbie exhaled.

'Do you think he'll come here? Hadleigh, I mean.'

'No-one knows you're here. And, if he did somehow find out – look around you. There are seven of us, and one of him.' Jan squeezed her arm. 'You're safe here. So are your daughters.'

'Did Mark tell you Hadleigh had someone follow them home from school one day?' Debbie shuddered. 'I was terrified at first. And then, when I had time to think about it some more, I got angry. Really angry. I wanted to find him and hurt him. Do anything to stop him.'

A stream of voices bursting from the radio made them both jump, and Jan turned from the woman as Carl Ansty turned up the volume and held up his hand for silence as he listened.

His face turned pale as the news filtered through, Kennedy's barked orders carrying over the airwaves.

'Did… did he just say that Mark's house has been firebombed?' Jan moved to the table, straining to hear over the excited voices in the kitchen while Antsy took notes and relayed orders to his wider team in the lanes around the safe house.

'He's okay.' Alex was holding his mobile phone, Caroline peering over his shoulder and reading out the text. 'He says Hadleigh put a petrol bomb through the front window. They're all safe, and there are two fire engines on site. The blaze is under control.'

'I'll head over there,' said Jan, lifting her coat off the back of one of the chairs and shrugging it over her shoulders. She flipped her hair over the collar. 'You both stay here with the rest of the team, just in case that was a ruse to divert our attention away from the safe house.'

Frowning, she cast her gaze over the table, then moved to the worktop and lifted the newspapers and magazines that had been discarded over the course of the night shift.

'Has anyone seen my car keys?'

A flutter of negative responses met her question, and she crossed to where she had left her handbag next to the kettle, rummaging through the pockets with an increased sense of urgency.

'Where's Debbie?'

Jan spun around at Alex's question, realised the woman was no longer in the kitchen, and rushed to the hallway.

'Debbie?' she called up the stairs.

She spotted bare legs through the railings that ran along the landing before Louise peered over, her brow creased.

'Where's Mum?'

Forcing a smile, Jan waved the girl back to her room. 'Here, somewhere. Look after your sister, okay?'

The teenager disappeared from sight, but Jan couldn't prevent the wave of panic that surged through her veins and punched her in the chest as she wrenched open the front door.

Her car was missing.

'Shit.'

CHAPTER FIFTY

Mark had been hovering at the periphery of the front garden when the firefighting team began dousing the flames from his living room and wrestling the blaze under control.

It hadn't taken long.

Within minutes the fire was reduced to smoking ashes and, ignoring a shout from the lead fire officer, he stalked across the soaking wet lawn to the front door.

None of the fire crew had reported seeing a man fleeing the scene, their attention instead on getting to the property as fast as possible and making it safe.

Nevertheless, the hairs on the back of Mark's neck prickled, the sense that Hadleigh wasn't finished with him yet making him unwilling to stand back and let others take control of the situation.

The petrol-fuelled flames had burned through the ceiling of the living room, melting through wiring and destroying his books and vinyl record collection, the television and anything else that stood in its way.

All that was left of his two-seater sofa and armchairs was a sorry pile of charred wood and smoking, sodden stuffing that belched chemical fumes into the air and made his eyes water.

He looked away, blinking to clear his vision, and cast his gaze across the concrete path that led back to the gate cut into the privet hedge that bordered the pavement.

He beckoned to PC Alice Fields, who had turned up with the first responders.

'What's up, Sarge?'

Mark pointed to the paving slab beside the gate post. 'This. The water from the hoses has washed away most of it.'

Alice crouched and wrinkled her nose, then looked up at him. 'Blood spatter?'

'He's been injured,' said Mark, pointing out the blood trail that led back towards the house. 'Badly, too.'

Alice turned. 'Then where is he?'

Mark squinted against the morning sun and shielded his eyes with his hands. 'He couldn't have gone far. The milk van's still here.'

'Why not use that?'

'Too obvious perhaps.' Mark peered inside the driver's cab. 'Look – there's blood all over the seat and steering wheel, too. Maybe he's so badly hurt, he can't drive it anymore. Get one of those uniform teams to start looking for the driver. Hadleigh must've overpowered him and left him somewhere nearby,' said Mark, then spun on his heel.

'Sarge? Where are you going?'

'To find the bastard who petrol-bombed my house,' he snarled. 'Like you said, he couldn't have gone far.'

He took off at a sprint, but slowed as he left the cul-de-sac and then stopped at the junction with the main road.

Cars were now streaming past at regular intervals but he ignored the passing traffic and swept his eyes across the pavement.

There – over by the signpost that named the street leading to the cul-de-sac, was what he was searching for.

Another splatter of blood – more this time, as if Hadleigh had paused to rest a moment and tried to stem the bleeding.

Mark paced back and forth, trying to figure out which way the man had gone next, then heard the honk of a car horn from further up the road, in the opposite direction from the town centre, and picked up his pace.

Sure enough, a few spots of blood splashed across the pavement here and there, and Mark imagined Hadleigh holding his hand to his chest as he hurried away from the crime scene, trying to stem the flow of blood.

Perhaps he had cut himself when breaking the window or throwing the petrol bomb. Given the amount of blood, his injury was deep enough that he would need urgent medical attention – and soon.

Yet he couldn't, could he?

Not without giving up. Not without handing himself in to face the consequences of the murders he had sanctioned or committed.

A grim satisfaction gripped Mark with the knowledge that because Hadleigh had murdered everyone who might have given him up under police questioning, he had isolated himself, leaving him nowhere to turn for help.

The thought made him pick up his pace, determined to find the man who had tried to take his life and destroy his career.

His breathing was heavy now – not from exertion, but from the panic that rose in his chest.

He wanted to be the one to stop Hadleigh. He wanted to be the one to slip the cuffs over his wrists, read him his rights, and then watch the man across the table in one of the interview rooms as he informed him what was going to happen next.

Because Mark would make damn sure the man received a life sentence.

Maybe two.

He wouldn't rest until he knew Matthew's killer was put away for a long time.

There were more car horns, and he saw

worried expressions in the faces of drivers that passed by.

Hadleigh's injury must have been bad enough to draw attention, and a renewed sense of urgency gripped Mark.

He broke into a run, following the blood stains that now appeared on a more regular basis.

He couldn't afford for Hadleigh to bleed out before he reached him.

There!

Up ahead, Mark spotted Hadleigh lurching from side to side as he staggered forwards, trying to make his escape.

The man was hunched over, his right hand clutched to his chest, blood stains covering his blue denim jeans. As if sensing Mark's approach, he glanced over his shoulder and scowled, then tried to increase his pace.

The arrogance and swagger Mark had associated with Hadleigh had disappeared – in its place was the stumbling lurching figure of a desperate man.

A roundabout lay ahead, splitting the road four ways. As Mark ran, he dug his mobile phone from his pocket, unlocked it, peered at the screen and toggled the recent calls list until he found Kennedy's name and pressed it.

'Hadleigh!'

The man glanced over his shoulder, eyes manic. Instead of slowing, he seemed to force a new burst of energy from his body and surged forward.

'Mark? Where the hell are you?'

'Radley Road, guv – heading towards the roundabout at the junction with Twelve Acre Drive. Can you get a couple of cars and an ambulance here? Hadleigh is injured – badly, I think – he's going to need urgent medical attention.'

'Have you apprehended him?'

'Not yet. Working on it.'

Mark ended the call as Hadleigh stopped.

He leaned forward and rested a hand on one of his knees, his shoulders heaving.

'Got you, you bastard.' Mark slowed to a walk, a stitch beginning to twist the muscles between his ribs. Raising his voice, he tucked the phone in his back pocket. 'Give it up, Hadleigh. You need to get to a hospital. Now.'

'Fuck off, Turpin.'

The man's voice sounded weak, despite the forced defiance. He straightened, his face contorting as he looked down at his hand, blood streaming from a wound that Mark could now see carved into his palm.

Mark heard voices, and looked behind to see a woman walking her dog on the opposite side of the road, her forehead creased as she stared at the strange man bleeding all over the pavement.

A group of three schoolboys in smart blazers and sports bags over their shoulders jeered and gesticulated, all bravado while they pulled out phones and began to take pictures.

'Shit.' Mark turned his attention back to Hadleigh. 'Sit on the pavement. Raise your hand above your head. It'll help stem the bleeding.'

'Fuck you.'

'Why'd you kill Matthew? He was only a kid.' Mark took a step closer. 'Why did he come here?'

Hadleigh took a step backwards. 'Stay where you are, Turpin.'

'Okay, okay.' Mark held up his hands. 'So? Are you going to tell me?'

'Stupid little shit was going to blow the whole operation out the water.' Hadleigh spat, the globule of phlegm smacking the pavement inches from Mark's feet.

He didn't move, and instead held Hadleigh's glare.

'Matthew decided he wanted out, and he remembered your face from last time. So, when he saw your photo in all the papers, I guess he thought you could help him. Problem was, we were expanding the supply chain this way. If he'd spoken to you, eighteen months' worth of work would've gone up in smoke.' Hadleigh shook his head, choking out a bitter laugh. 'All that work – gone, thanks to a fourteen-year-old kid who decided to grow a conscience.'

'I guess he grew up.'

'He was a pain in the arse.'

'So you had Shaun Mansell murder him. Why kill Shaun and Dean?'

'Why not?' Hadleigh shrugged. 'Collateral damage. Shaun was going to talk to you lot after he killed Matty. Dean was a loose end. They both served a purpose, that's all.'

'You tried to kill my family.'

Hadleigh sneered. 'More's the pity when I

found out they weren't on board. Nice little reunion you had on the towpath, was it?'

'Why even bring them into this? This was never about them – it was always between you and me.'

'To send you a message of course. Then, when I realised you had moved in together, I figured it'd corral you all into that house. I could take you all out in one go then and be sure to do it properly this time—'

'Yeah – about that,' said Mark. He took a step closer, unable to keep the smugness from his voice. 'You failed, Hadleigh. My family weren't in the house. We moved them away so you couldn't harm them. And those of us left in the house are all alive.'

The blare of sirens cut through the shocked silence that followed his words.

'D'you hear that, Hadleigh? They're coming here to save you because I'm going to make sure you live,' Mark spat. 'And then, I'm going to make sure a judge puts you away for a very long time. With any luck, you won't be out this side of your seventieth birthday.'

Hadleigh cackled. 'Like I said, fuck you, Turpin.'

He pressed his hand back against his chest, then turned to run across the road.

'No – stop!' Mark yelled.

Too late, Hadleigh reacted.

He took a step back, as if surprised by the proximity of the car bearing down on him, and then his body was catapulted into the air, somersaulting across the windscreen before landing on the kerb in a crumpled broken heap.

A silence fell on the road, as if time had stopped.

The woman who had been walking her dog only moments earlier stood frozen in place, shock emanating from her. The dog whined.

The schoolboys lowered their phones to stare at the still form lying in the middle of the street, faces stricken.

Mark held his breath, waiting for Hadleigh to move, waiting for the screaming to begin.

Nothing happened.

He began to run then, pulling out his mobile phone and calling in the accident as he slid to a standstill beside Hadleigh and crouched, fingers moving to the man's neck before he tried to locate a heartbeat he knew he wouldn't find.

Rising on shaking legs, he waved away the onlookers, told them to wait further along the road at a junction with a dead end street. He could hear the sirens approaching now; the occupants of those cars could take the statements that would be needed.

The driver...

He spun around as the car door swung open, and a woman emerged, eyes wide in a pale face, her hand moving to her mouth.

Mark's heart missed a beat.

'Debbie? What are you doing here?'

CHAPTER FIFTY-ONE

Mark eyed the paper bag that Jan placed on the low wooden table in front of him, and then looked at his colleague.

She shrugged. 'Figured you probably hadn't eaten this morning.'

The fatty aroma of fried food made his mouth water, and he snatched up the bag, ripped it open and sank his teeth into the thick pie crust.

'Oh my God, that's good,' he said, wiping a trace of gravy from his lips with a paper napkin. 'You're a saint.'

'I know.'

Their voices echoed within the empty

confines of the atrium, the rest of the station busy at desks around the building or out on call.

Mark leaned back in the chair, reached out for the television remote and muted the sound. 'What's happening upstairs?'

'It's bedlam, as you can imagine.'

'Is the Chief Super still here?'

'And will be for a while.'

'Shit. I hope Kennedy's not in too much trouble.'

'Not as much as you.' Jan smiled, then dropped onto the sofa next to him as he finished his pie. 'How are you holding up?'

He swallowed. 'It helps knowing Debbie will be allowed back home with the girls later on today. I think Gillian's going with her. At least they'll be in familiar surroundings while all this is going on.'

'What did Kennedy say will happen to her?'

'She's given a formal statement.' He balled up the paper bag and tossed it onto the table. 'I don't think they'll charge her with dangerous driving or anything like that – she had nowhere to go; Hadleigh stepped right out in front of her, and there are witnesses to corroborate her version of events.'

'The dog walker and the school kids?'

'Exactly.'

'And you?' She gave him a nudge. 'Don't think you're going to get away with avoiding the question.'

Mark sighed. 'Honestly? I'm glad it's over. I wish my family had never got dragged into this. I wish Matthew hadn't been used like he was, then killed because he tried to get help.'

'Do you wish Hadleigh had lived so he could face a court and be sentenced?'

'No.' He could hear the vehemence in his voice, and cleared his throat. 'Although I should probably say I do. But after what he did to all those people, and what he had planned for Abingdon with those drugs, I'm glad he's dead.'

'Me too.' Jan smiled. 'So, given that you're persona non grata upstairs for the foreseeable future, do you want an off-the-record update?'

'I thought you'd never ask. Go on, then.'

His colleague checked over her shoulder as two administrative assistants walked past, then lowered her voice. 'The milkman was found in a shallow ditch bordering the Radley Road half an hour after the ambulance left your position. Hadleigh had slashed his chest and stomach when he pulled him from the float, but he's going to live, according to the surgeon who operated on him a couple of hours ago.'

Mark exhaled, running a hand over his face. 'That's something, at least. Did he say what happened?'

'Hadleigh took him by surprise. He'd climbed back into the float after a delivery along there, and was about to drive off when Hadleigh emerged and wrenched open the driver's door. The driver smashed a bottle and lashed out at Hadleigh, cutting his hand before he pulled him out into the road. He managed to get to his feet and went to wrestle Hadleigh, but that's when he got stabbed. Hadleigh pushed him into the hedge before driving off. You didn't see him when you were chasing after Hadleigh a while later, because he'd stumbled and fallen into that ditch. He thinks he passed out for a while – when he heard sirens, he came to and managed to crawl out and flag down a passing motorist.'

'Poor bugger. What about the teenager who

was made to drive Hadleigh's car and lead you lot on a goose chase? Didn't I hear that Hadleigh threatened his girlfriend?'

'We found her safe and well at home – they rent a cottage on the outskirts of Challow. Caroline and Alex went over and took their statements earlier this afternoon. As you can imagine, the lad who was driving is still shaken up. The doctor at the hospital gave him a clean bill of health though – no whiplash or anything like that from the crash.'

'Glad to hear it.' Mark peered at his phone as it emitted a single bleep, and smiled.

'Lucy?'

'Yes. I'm meant to be meeting her in a half an hour.'

'Best get a move on then, Sarge, instead of sitting around here moping.' Jan grinned. 'Are you two going to be all right after all this?'

He nodded. 'I think so, yes. I hope so, anyway.'

Rising from the sofa with an ill-disguised groan, Mark put on his jacket and shoved his hands in his pockets.

'Come on, Sarge. Don't look so despondent,'

said Jan, her tone light. 'This suspension will probably only be short-term, just while they sort out all the paperwork and work out what they're going to say to Professional Standards.'

'You think so?'

'You just put yourself on the line to solve a murder investigation involving three victims. They're not going to let you go after this, are they?'

He grimaced. 'I hope not. I've kind of got used to it here.'

CHAPTER FIFTY-TWO

Two days later

Mark paused at the gated entrance to the boatyard, the wind tugging at his hair.

The day promised to be one that he would remember for many years, and despite the week's events and the subsequent suspension from duties, he wanted to spend a moment savouring the anticipation of what would come next.

He checked his phone once more, then put it away.

Lucy had said she would be here, and he had to stop worrying.

The past twenty-four hours had been busy – his landlord had refused to renegotiate his lease, none of the other tenancy agencies in the area would even speak to him, and Lucy had spent the previous day making some urgent enquiries about their options.

His heart missed a beat at the sound of a familiar car engine, and then a small hatchback slowed before turning into the concrete apron outside the marina.

Lucy emerged, slung her handbag over her shoulder and flicked her curls from her face, then wandered over to join him, turning the keys to James's car in her hands. Her smile widened as he drew her into a hug.

'Did you let him know I'll give him some cash towards the fuel yesterday?'

'He said not to worry about it.' She drew away and peered at the different sized boats lining the yard. 'Ready?'

'As ready as I'll ever be.'

'Come on then.'

She slipped her hand into his and led him

through the open steel gates towards the door of the chandler's office, a wooden-slatted cabin that took up a corner of the yard.

The sound of power tools echoed from a barn-sized shed to the right of it, and Mark noticed the camber of the concrete change as the yard sloped down towards the river's edge.

'Have you spoken to Debbie?' Lucy's voice cut through his thoughts. 'I was wondering how they were getting on.'

'She's getting there. I think it'll take a while. Thank goodness Gillian has put her in touch with a counsellor.' He shivered. 'I think she's going to need it after the accident and everything else.'

'And the girls?'

'Relieved to be home, but none the worse for wear.'

'Will you see them again?'

'Yes – Debbie has already said that won't be a problem. We'll just see how things go over the next few weeks first.'

'She's forgiven you, then?'

'Forgiven, not forgotten.' Mark shrugged. 'It's the best I can hope for at the moment, at least.'

Holding open the door into the chandler's

office for her, he stopped on the threshold for a moment to let his eyes adjust to the gloom compared to outside.

A moment later, a stocky man in his sixties emerged from a door off to the left. He gripped Lucy's hand, and to Mark's surprise gave her a hug before turning to him.

'Brian Croft,' he said, then nodded at Lucy. 'I've known this one for years – I couldn't believe it when I heard what happened to her boat. None of us could.'

Mark returned the handshake. 'She's told me a lot about you over the past couple of days.'

'All good, I hope.' Croft winked, then gestured to a paperwork-strewn desk and a dusty laptop. 'Take a seat. Thanks for emailing the particulars through, Lucy – that'll save us some time.'

'Not a problem at all, Brian. Thanks for making it such an easy process.'

'Least we could do. Hang on.' He rummaged amongst a short stack of manila folders on his desk, then drew out one from near the top of the pile, opening it and passing a document to Lucy before settling into his chair and folding his hands on the desk. 'Okay, here's the contract as agreed. The specifications are attached to the back, but it's the seventy-foot model – perfect for when you have guests staying – and it's got the additional headroom for you, Mark. We'll bring it down from Oxford for you early next week and give it a thorough check over as well as making the minor modifications you've requested, but you should be able to take delivery a week today.'

'Fabulous, thanks,' said Lucy.

Mark perched on the edge of his seat, unable to tear his gaze from the contract.

They had stayed up late into the night on Thursday, unable to sleep in the hotel room that he had booked, their words tumbling over each other's as they had talked through the events that had first thrown them together, then brought them closer.

Mark had sat down and drawn up a list of what belongings he had left after the fire, before deciding he didn't need half of them, and Lucy had ruefully pointed out that she would be starting from scratch.

Downsizing had seemed the most sensible option in the circumstances.

Now, Lucy's pen hovered over the contract, and Mark noticed her hand shaking.

As if sensing his eyes on her, she glanced up, her eyebrow raised. 'Are you sure?'

'Sign away,' he said, and winked.

She grinned, executed her signature with a flourish, and then slid the paperwork over to him.

After he had counter-signed the contract, he lowered the pen to the desk, a sense of wonder clutching at his chest. 'We've just bought a bloody boat.'

Lucy emitted a nervous laugh. 'A bloody *big* boat.'

'Congratulations, both of you. You're going to love it,' said Croft. He took back the contract, added his signature and then pushed back his chair. 'I'll get a photocopy of this for you to take with you, and we'll send you a copy by email as well. Back in a minute.'

Mark waited until the marina owner had left the room, then pushed back his chair and pulled Lucy into a hug.

'I love you.'

'Love you, too.'

His mobile phone began to ring.

'That can't be work,' said Lucy. 'They're not talking to you at the moment, are they?'

Pulling out the phone from his jeans pocket, he frowned. 'I don't recognise the number. It's a local one, though. Hello?'

'Hello? Is that Mark Turpin?'

'Yes.'

'It's Natalie over at the Culham veterinary surgery here. I don't want to raise your hopes, but a woman brought in a dog to us a few days ago. One of my receptionists read in the local paper today about what happened with the boat fire and your dog going missing, and we wondered if he might be yours. Would you be prepared to come over to the practice and have a look at him?'

Mark swallowed, and glanced at Lucy, who was looking at him with concern in her eyes.

'What is it?' she said, frowning.

He shook his head and turned his attention back to the caller. 'Of – of course. Where are you?'

Moving to the desk and tearing a page from a notepad before picking up the pen they had used to sign the contract, he took down the address, and then ended the call.

'Mark? What's going on?'

He turned to see both Lucy and Croft staring at him with confused expressions.

'They think they've found Hamish.'

————

Lucy didn't trust Mark to drive her neighbour's car from the marina to Culham, so instead Mark sat in the passenger seat and resisted the urge to stomp his foot on a non-existent accelerator as she negotiated her way along the twisting roads towards the veterinary surgery.

The twenty-year-old practice took up a building that had once been a dentist's surgery, which in turn had once been a large family residence on the outskirts of a village quickly being consumed by a large industrial park to the south.

Lucy had barely touched the brakes upon pulling up to the kerb outside before Mark threw open the car door and hurried through a gap in the red-brick wall and up to the front door.

She grinned as he remembered to wait for her on the doorstep.

'Just remember what you told me she'd said on the phone,' she reminded him as he opened the door. 'Don't get your hopes up, all right?'

'Like you're not,' he murmured, then turned his attention to the receptionist who peered at them from across a dark-coloured wooden desk. 'We're here to see Natalie. She phoned me earlier about a dog that had been found abandoned.'

'Ah, the Schnauzer cross.' The woman smiled, and pressed a button on the telephone beside her computer. 'Right – that's diverted through to our other surgery in town for a minute. I'm glad she got in touch. I'm Tamsin – Natalie's just gone out to do a home visit.'

'Where was he found?' Mark gave her a smile, aware of the urgency in his tone. All he wanted to do was find out if they had really found Hamish, not make small talk.

'A woman was walking her dog along the towpath beyond Abingdon Lock and heard him whining,' she said. 'Her dog ran off in the direction of the sound, and when she found him, the little dog was lying next to a tree with some old rope wrapped around his collar. He'd tried to gnaw through it by the look of it, but it was too thick. He's got some nasty lacerations in his neck from where he'd tried to break free, but we've cleaned those up and there's no sign of infection. He's dehydrated more than anything.'

'Thank God she heard him,' said Lucy.

'At least she did. He seems to be recovering well, anyway. Come on through.'

She led the way through a door and along a short corridor with consulting rooms off each side of it, then through into an inner room that was lined with large cages.

'This is our recovery room,' she said, lowering her voice. 'It's where our overnight stays are kept for observation post-operation, as well as those like this dog who have been rescued and need extra attention.'

Mark kept his eyes averted from the tiny forms in the blankets within two of the cages, and followed Tamsin to the corner of the room.

She crouched next to the cage and opened the door before looking over her shoulder.

'Here you go.'

Taking a deep breath, unsure what he would see, Mark squeezed Lucy's hand before they lowered themselves to the floor and peered in.

'Hamish?'

Sleepy eyes peered out at him from a cocoon of pale-green blankets, before a familiar *yip* and a tail wag sent an IV drip crashing against the side of the cage.

'Steady, boy,' murmured Tamsin. She lowered her head before checking the dog's bandaged paw.

'What's that?' said Lucy, her voice shaking.

'Just some fluids and some antibiotics to keep any infections at bay.'

She moved out of the way, and Mark dropped to his stomach so he could reach in and stroke Hamish's head.

'How're you doing?' he murmured, his throat thick as he blinked back tears. 'What did they do to you, eh?'

A nose brushed against his palm in response, and then a tongue rasped across his fingers.

Mark gave a shaky laugh, his hand trembling as he ruffled Hamish's ears.

The dog blinked, then yawned, and burrowed his nose into the blankets.

Tamsin smiled as Mark extricated himself from the cage. 'I take it he's yours?'

'Yes, yes he is,' he said. He sat back on his

heels as Lucy reached into the cage and made a fuss of Hamish, her voice cooing under her breath. 'When can we take him home?'

'In a few days,' said Tamsin, 'and if I could make a suggestion? Let us microchip him before you do. At least that way you'll find each other a bit faster if he escapes.'

'I will.' Mark bit back a choke and squeezed Lucy's shoulder as Hamish sidled closer and licked her fingers.

'I'm never going to let either of them out of my sight again.'

THE END

ABOUT THE AUTHOR

Rachel Amphlett is a USA Today bestselling author of crime fiction and spy thrillers, many of which have been translated worldwide.

Her novels are available in eBook, print, and audiobook formats from libraries and retailers as well as her website shop.

A keen traveller, Rachel has both Australian and British citizenship.

Find out more about Rachel's books at: www.rachelamphlett.com.